Ella Rodman Church

In the Hospital at Elmridge

Ella Rodman Church

In the Hospital at Elmridge

ISBN/EAN: 9783337161330

Printed in Europe, USA, Canada, Australia, Japan

Cover: Foto ©Andreas Hilbeck / pixelio.de

More available books at **www.hansebooks.com**

BY

ELLA RODMAN CHURCH,

AUTHOR OF "BIRDS AND THEIR WAYS," "FLYERS AND CRAWLERS,"
"FLOWER-TALKS AT ELMRIDGE," ETC.

———•———

PHILADELPHIA :
PRESBYTERIAN BOARD OF PUBLICATION
AND SABBATH-SCHOOL WORK,
No. 1334 CHESTNUT STREET.

WESTCOTT & THOMSON,
Stereotypers and Electrotypers, Philada.

CONTENTS.

CHAPTER IX.

CHAPTER X.

CHAPTER XI.

CHAPTER XII.

CHAPTER XIII.

CHAPTER XIV.

CHAPTER XV.

CHAPTER XVI.

CHAPTER XVII.

CHAPTER XVIII.

INTRODUCTION.

In the "Elmridge Series" the author has given to the public, through the Presbyterian Board of Publication, *Birds and their Ways*, which is full of interesting facts and information about the birds of the air; *Flyers and Crawlers*, which tells about the world of insects; *Flower-Talks at Elmridge*, in which we have delightful talks about flowers; *Among the Trees at Elmridge*, a volume that introduces us to the trees; and *Talks by the Seashore*, in which we are conducted beneath the waves of the ocean and learn much about the strange creatures that live there. In the present volume the young people and their governess, with whom we have become so well acquainted, meet with an unwelcome interruption in their studies, which, however, leads to scenes of novel interest, and to the study of a fresh subject while they are *In the Hospital at Elmridge.*

In the Hospital at Elmridge.

CHAPTER I.

THE HOSPITAL.

IT may seem rather odd, after taking the little Kyles to the seashore, where they had those pleasant "talks,"* to put them all the way back in the midst of the measles, which they had had the winter before. But some other little people who heard of their seashore doings wanted very much to know how they acted when they were sick, and especially how Miss Harson acted; for they were quite sure that she had done some particularly nice things. In this, as you will see, they were not mistaken. The poor children really had a very tedious time of it, for, as Dr. Gates pleasantly said, "they seemed to take all the measles that were to

* *Talks by the Seashore.* Presbyterian Board of Publication.

be had," and they were very slow about getting well again.   It was this slowness that
took them to the seashore.

The trouble began very mildly indeed;
so that at first no one thought much of it.
Edith, who was a delicate little girl and
rather enjoyed being just ill enough to
have her breakfast in bed and to be generally petted—"just comfortably sick," papa
called it—said one morning that her head
ached and she did not care about getting up.

"I know what that means," laughed her
governess as she looked in upon the little
invalid; "it means that Kitty is to put
something nice in the rose bowl—cream-
toast, I shouldn't wonder—and a bunch
of white grapes on the prettiest plate;
and when all has been cleared away, the
dolls must be set in a row, and Clara must
devote herself to amusing you until I can
tell you a story.   I see that we are going
to have a regular day of it."

"I don't think I want anything to eat,"
said Edie, languidly; and Miss Harson
found that the little girl's head and hands
were quite hot.

The cream-toast came up in due time, and the dainty china bowl with great pink roses over it ; but, although Kitty's cream-toast was something quite different from common, the little girl could eat only a tiny piece, and she fairly turned away from the grapes.

Mr. Kyle came in to see his little daughter before he went to the city ; but he was not a doctor, and he only said, as he laid his hand on her brow and smoothed back the golden hair,

" She is a little feverish, I think, and had better keep quiet to-day. She probably has eaten something that disagrees with her, but she will be all right again to-morrow.—Good-bye, darling."

The next moment the jingling of the sleigh-bells told them that papa was on his way to the station, but, for some reason or other, Edith began to cry at the sound, and it was some time before she could be quieted.

Morning had vanished into afternoon and afternoon into twilight, and still the little girl did not wish to get up and be dressed. She made no complaint except that her head ached and she did not like the sunshine, but Miss Harson bathed the aching head with cool water and then with cologne, and shaded the glare on the snow from her eyes, until Edith finally dropped off asleep. She slept on heavily, and did not waken again during the night.

"Oh, Miss Harson," exclaimed Clara, the next morning, as she rushed excitedly into her governess's room, "please come and look at Edie; she's all over red spots."

Miss Harson ran with a quickly-beating heart, for she feared all sorts of dreadful things; but a glance at Edith's crimson face and swollen eyes made her guess the truth. She did not think it was anything worse than measles, and, although this was bad enough, she felt relieved.

Dr. Gates was sent for, and came at once, and he said it was measles; and that settled the matter.

"Looks a little serious just now," he said to Mr. Kyle at the front door, "but I think that with good nursing she'll pull through."

"I suppose the other children must be

kept away from her?" asked Mr. Kyle. ."And this will be very hard for them all."

"No," replied the doctor; "the girl will have it, any way—in fact, she's got it now— and let the boy take his chance."

Yes, Clara too was drooping and com- plained of a headache; but when Edie whispered, "Won't it be nice for us both to be sick together?" she did not like the idea at all, and declared that she "*wouldn't* be sick." The next morning she did not feel very well, and she lay looking curiously at her little sister, until, seeing Edith's eyes open and fixed on her, she said, not very wisely,

"You *do* look so funny, Edie! Just like a speckled hen."

"So do *you*," was the reply; "I guess you look worser than I do. You aren't pretty a bit."

"Not pretty"! This was rather more than Clara could stand; and from her own sister too! and she began to cry violently. Then Edie cried because Clara did, and Miss Har- son came in to find two red-faced, tearful- eyed little girls who were sick and cross and not easy to pacify. But the cool hands and loving tones and gentle movements had a very soothing effect, and after a while the two flushed faces rested quietly on their pillows and the heavy eyelids were closed.

This is the way in which Clara and Edith began to have the measles.

For a week or ten days the large house at Elmridge was very quiet, and the large room in which the two little sisters lay, each in her own white bed, was kept quite dark. They were having it hard, the doctor said, and it was necessary to be very careful. Jane had become their devoted nurse—a sister of hers having come to do her usual work—and this relieved Miss Harson, who could now attend to the comfort of her little charges without being wearied out. So many things as she found to do for them in addition to what Jane did! and, now that they would soon be able to have more light in the room, a beautiful plan came into her head.

But first you must know that St. John's

Hospital in Brooklyn is a lovely place for sick people of all ages, and especially for sick children. A great, sunshiny room which is called "The Children's Ward" has several immense windows that seem to bathe the little beds in a constant stream of light, and there are climbing plants and beautiful flowers and verses of Scripture painted on the walls. The beds are so white and the floor is so clean and the faces of the ladies who take care of the sick children are so sweet and smiling that it is no wonder some of the poor suffering little waifs who are taken there ask if they are in heaven.

Elmridge was not so far away but that Miss Harson could in a few hours take her little pupils to the hospital to visit the sick children there and bring them back. How the little prisoners in bed loved to see them come! There were sure to be oranges and other dainties which the doctors would allow them to eat, but it was best of all just to have the little Kyles bring themselves. They were always so bright and pleasant, and so nice in all the

wards that even the grown-up people clam-
ored for them, and the child-patients were
simply delighted.

Many of these sick little ones had names
that were quite different from those which
were given to them in infancy, and the
young Elmridgers were at first quite
puzzled over " Little Brown-Eyes," " Little
Grandmother," and some others of whom
we shall hear by and by. It was not long,
however, before they could give each patient her right name, and they learned to
love them all very much. Most of the sick
children were girls. Sometimes a very tiny
boy was seen in the ward, but the real Boys'
Ward was in another room. It was not so
pretty a room as the Children's Ward, and
there were never many boys in it; but it
looked sweet, clean and peaceful, like all
the rest of the house, and the boys who
went there seemed to get well fast.

Miss Harson's plan for a home-hospital
seemed to require a great deal of help, although she carried out part of it in her own
room; but while the children slept Thomas

came in very quietly, carrying vines and plants, which he put just where the young lady directed him to, and then, with his assistance, some beautiful painted mottoes appeared like magic on the walls. The little patients noticed these things by degrees, for at first they were too ill to be surprised at anything; but by and by it dawned upon them that their room had grown wonderfully like the Children's Ward in the hospital. Their kind governess had certainly spared no pains to make it as much like the hospital as possible, and to carry out the idea she had even collected all the dolls belonging to Clara and Edith —a tolerably large family—and had them ranged along the wall, each in a little bed, as though they too were sick. Of course not every doll had a bed of her own, but several of them had, and where no bedstead could be found to match a doll Miss Harson went to work and made one of pasteboard, prettily painted; and when it was put in place along with the other beds, with nice little sheets and counterpane and a cunning little pillow—on which the dolly's

head appeared to be so very comfortable
—it was certainly a close imitation of the
real thing.

It was such a pretty room in itself that
the two little sisters had, with three windows in it; and the two single bedsteads,
just alike, were made of a beautiful light
wood called "natural cherry." The low,
straight headboards and footboards were
carved with rosebuds and leaves, and the
carpet was thickly covered with pink rosebuds and green leaves that looked as natural as if some one had just passed through
the room with a large basketful of buds and
leaves and scattered them over the floor.
There were two small bureaus to match the
bedsteads, two tables and several low, pretty
chairs, and on the walls were pictures of
children and a large colored photograph of
the dear mamma who had left this beautiful
home and gone to paradise three years ago.
This picture was still wreathed with a
Christmas garland, and at Easter the
choicest flowers were always placed around
it. The curtains to the windows were of
cream-colored Canton flannel, looped back

with blue ribbons, and in the small low-
down grate a cheery fire was burning

It was certainly a very pleasant room for
a hospital, and this is what Clara thought
one morning when she awoke feeling very
much better. For a few moments she lay
perfectly still, looking around, and then she
began to smile. That dear Miss Harson!
how much she must have done in the night!
The two beds occupied by the live patients
were near the centre of the room, with their
heads against the wall and not very far
apart, while on the farther side of each
bed, ranging down to the opposite walls
of the room, was a row of dolls' beds,
seven or eight in each row, and it seemed
to Clara that all the dolls they had ever
known and almost forgotten were lying in
those beds. How cunning they looked,
too! just like a real hospital; and there
was her own beautiful brand-new Isabel,
named after her beloved governess—did
any one ever have a lovelier name?—that
came to her only at Christmas, close beside
her and gazing up with those starry brown
eyes (she was so glad they were not blue,

2

like most of the other dolls'), while her real
hair, just the color of Edie's, floated away
from her waxen face in careless waves and
curls.   She was a splendid armful, this immense, beautifully-made doll—about as much
as her young mother could carry when she
was well and strong, and now she could
only lie and look at her.   She was dressed
like a very little girl, in white, with some
pretty lace trimming and a broad blue sash;
she had also light-blue silk stockings tied
with blue satin ribbon, and the daintiest of
bronze-kid boots.   She was just the delight
of Clara's eyes, who had asked particularly
for such a doll as one of her Christmas gifts,
and she seemed so real that while the little
girl was admiring the soft rose-tint of her
cheek she actually found herself hoping
that the doll would not catch the measles
and be made such a fright as *she* was.

Perhaps it was this that made Clara burst
out laughing, and presently she had wak-
ened Edie, who looked up with a faint
smile; for she too felt better.   But she
had been more ill than Clara, and it took
her longer to get strong again.

"Where are we?" asked the little one, feeling much bewildered as she glanced around. "Have we got into the hospital?"

"Yes, dear," was the soft reply as her governess bent over her, "into your own pretty room, that I have tried to make like the Children's Ward, which has always seemed so pleasant to you. Isn't it nice?"

Edith squeezed Miss Harson's hand quite vigorously for a sick little girl as she said,

"It's lovely, and I'm so glad to see all the plants and things. It makes me think of something besides being sick, you know."

This was just the effect Miss Harson wanted to produce when she made the changes, and she felt well paid for all her trouble.

"That's Clara's ward," continued the little girl, glancing at her sister's bed and the row of queer little patients beside it, "and this is mine; and we can both play at taking care of 'em. Have they all got measles, Miss Harson? or can they have something else?"

The young lady thought it would make a pleasanter variety to distribute a few other diseases among the dollies; so one had whooping-cough, and another scarlet-fever, a third rheumatism, and, having heard an old woman at the hospital say so of herself, Edith decided that there was nothing the matter with a fourth but old age. As this was supposed to be a children's ward, it was a rather funny idea, but no funnier, perhaps, than to have whooping-cough and scarlet-fever, as well as measles, lying amicably side by side.

"I'm so glad Rosaletta isn't having it hard," said Edith of her best-beloved doll beside her; "there are no spots at all on her face."

"That is the worst kind," replied Clara, sagely. "I heard Dr. Gates say, when he saw how we looked, that it was a very good thing for us that we should be so covered with spots, because it was dangerous not to have it come out."

"Never mind, dear," said Miss Harson, seeing the troubled face; "you can just as well play that Rosaletta is not having it at all, for not every one who is exposed to a disease catches it. That will leave you with a sufficiently large family of sick children to take care of."

"Well," was the cheerful reply, "that's just what I will do. But how could you think, Miss Harson, of so many nice things for us?—Just see, Clara! We've each got a little rocking-chair tied with blue ribbon, like the children in the ward, and the tables are close by our beds, like theirs, with vases and flowers in them. Isn't it nice?"

The little girls were constantly making discoveries and delighting in their hospital more and more. Vines of English ivy and parlor ivy had been arranged on brackets to trail around the pictures as well as to climb up and down from hanging-baskets, and the window-boxes had primroses and some lovely white and pink geraniums in bloom. There was a tall calla-lily with two blossoms and a bud on it, and altogether John, the gardener, had really been very generous in parting with his treasures. But what would not the whole household

do for the sick children, who were really
so good and lovable?

The fragrance of a box of mignonette
seemed just like violets, and delighted the
little invalids extremely. But, strange as
it may sound, a box that seemed to have in
it nothing but a little moss on top interested
them most, and the reason of this was that
Clara's bright eyes—which were ready for
use some time before Edith's—had made
the discovery that under the moss were
little green shoots that were growing with
all their might and main, in the greatest
possible hurry to ornament themselves
with waxen bell-shaped flowers of different colors on different plants, that would
fill the room with fragrance. It was such
a beautiful mystery to watch, and *these* flowers would be all their own.

"And you painted them all, Miss Harson?" said Clara, gazing at the texts that
were opposite their beds. "How very
kind it was of you, and how beautiful
they are!"

The text that hung on the wall opposite
Clara's bed was

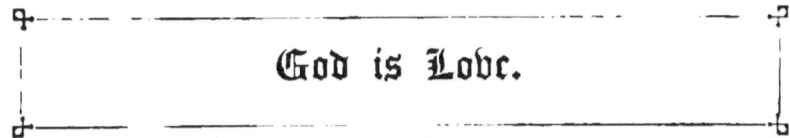

and that opposite Edie's was

$$\boxed{\text{𝕴 am the 𝕲ood 𝕾hepherd.}}$$

"I know that God loves us, Miss Harson," continued Clara, "because it says so in the Bible, and you have often told us so; but I do wonder just a little why he lets us be sick, then. Why do people have measles and things, when God can help it?"

Edith looked frightened, as though she expected her sister to be reproved for what she had said, but, instead of this, Miss Harson gently stroked the little hand she had taken in hers as she replied:

"My dear child, such questions have puzzled older heads than yours, and instead of answering them we can only rest on the words that are spoken to us by God himself—that 'God is love.' In another part of the Bible we are told that 'he ordereth all things well,' and in his wisdom he sees fit to send sickness to some of us, while others are left in health. But sickness and suffering also come to many who can get none of the comforts which make these things easier to bear, who are often without food or fire and can get none of the remedies which might restore them to health. How would it seem to you, for instance, if, instead of being here in your pleasant, luxurious room, you were really in a hospital—no matter how attractive a hospital—among other sick children in a ward? Would you not think then that children situated as you really are were about as happy as they could be and need not at all mind being sick?"

"Yes, indeed," exclaimed Clara. "I'd rather be here than at the hospital, except to visit."

"Yet you might easily be much worse off than to be in a hospital of any kind," continued her governess; "you might be tossing with fever on a wretched bed, with only some careless child, perhaps, left to watch you, because the others were obliged to go out to work, and often there would be no one to give you even a drink of water."

"How dreadful!" sighed Clara. "I should like to do something for such poor sick children, Miss Harson."

"Then, dear," whispered her governess, with shining eyes, "that may be the very reason why God saw fit to make you ill—that you might feel more for others. We will do some beautiful things, when you are able, to brighten the dreary sick days of children who have little love or care; but just now your only duty is to get well and strong."

"I like my text so much!" said Edith, gazing at the beautiful picture of "The Good Shepherd," which hung just over it. "Won't you tell us about some little lamb, Miss Harson, like that one the Saviour is carrying in his arms?"

"Yes, dear," was the reply, after a moment's thought. "I have a story that I wrote myself some time ago. In it there is something about a lamb; and if you are good and lie quite still now for a while, and do not let the plates go down stairs too full after your early dinner, I will read it to you."

It was difficult to tempt the delicate little patients' appetite with anything that was really good for them, but both now agreed to nibble a bit of the nice brown toast with a poached egg on it, which so many children would have been glad to get, and to drink a thimbleful or two of milk. But Dr. Gates said that they would not starve, because they drank a great deal of toast-water to quench their constant thirst; for there is nourishment in that.

This was the first story that Clara and Edith had been able to listen to for a great many days, and as, after dinner, the account of them was a pretty good one, they prepared themselves for a great treat. So Miss Harson seated herself between the two little beds and began to read

THE STORY OF JOE.

It was a very cold day—so cold, indeed, that everything looked frozen stiff and hard, and the few people who were out in the streets hurried by wrapped up to the eyes and seeming to glance neither to the right nor to the left. The car-drivers were swinging their arms vigorously to keep warm, and the poor horses nearly perished with cold. It was soon after the Christmas holidays, when the weather seems to be colder than at any other time of the year, and, while even the rich feel it, the poor are almost in despair.

Five o'clock in the afternoon is a cold time of day at this season, but a little boy who stood near the corner of a handsome square seemed to have forgotten how very cold it was. He was just in front of a grand stone church that had a straight, tapering spire of great height. Little Joe moved under one of the large windows, listening, and presently he exclaimed,

" Here they come !"

Then the sound of singing, that began far away, grew nearer and nearer. The chorister-boys were just passing into the church from a side-entrance, and they were very sweetly singing " Jerusalem the Golden." To the little boy out there in the cold it sounded like the song of angels, but a larger boy who had joined him was thinking of very different things.

"This is where the big-bugs come to church," said he as two or three ladies and gentlemen passed through the arched door- . way. "Don't I wish *I* was one of them, though! Come, Joe; let's you and me slip in along with 'em and git warm. They've got a big place in the floor there like the heater in the stores, only it's nicer, and there's pictures an' green wreaths, an' lots o' things; and if the sexton don't come down on us, we can stay till they've done prayers an' singin'."

"Go inside!" exclaimed Joe, with wild eyes; for, though he had often listened to the choristers, he had not thought of this. "Will they let the likes of *us?*"

"We won't ask 'em," was the easy reply; and Nick, the older and stronger boy, shuf- fled along to the door, dragging his com- panion with him. Once inside the vestibule, he peered cautiously around; but no sexton was to be seen, and soon he and Joe were warming their benumbed limbs over the register. This was near the large entrance-door, and as they stood there Joe gazed wonderingly up the grand aisle and studied the wide chancel-window, that had such beautiful pictures on it. In the centre was a figure of the blessed Saviour with a lamb folded in his arms, and on one side of the window there was a lamb carrying a banner with a cross on it. All this puzzled Joe very much, for he had never seen anything like it before, and there was no one to explain these symbols to the little wanderer.

But the boy's eyes lingered longest on the face of the Saviour, it was such a holy, loving face, and he wished that he had been the little lamb in his arms, to be gathered up so close and safe in his bosom. He did not know, you see, that the lambs the dear Saviour really folds in his bosom are just such stray waifs as himself.

In the chancel there were festoons and arches of evergreen, and all through the church, between the tall pillars that stood in a row on either side, were small hemlock trees just as they had been taken from the forest. Two or three clergymen and the

chorister-boys, all in white surplices, were
in the chancel, and those of the congrega-
tion who loved to join in the church-service
at that closing hour of the day were scattered among the pews.

The warmth and music and the beautiful
things around him made Joe feel as though
he were in heaven, and as he watched the
chorister-boys—some of whom were even
smaller than himself—he wondered if they
were like other boys, or if they were an
especial race by themselves. It was well
that he did not see them closely, for some
of them appeared quite unconscious of the
holy words they were singing, and laughed
and made faces at each other whenever they
thought they were not observed.

Joe tried to listen to the prayers and the
lessons of Scripture, but he was too far off
to hear very well, and he took more pleasure in the singing.

When the service was over, the choristers
walked down the aisle two by two, singing
the carol " Star of Wonder, Star of Night,"
and as their clear voices died away in the
distance little Joe heaved a deep sigh, for he

thought he would have liked to stay there for ever listening to them. For this poor boy had no one to tell him of the more beautiful songs of heaven; he had no warm, comfortable home to go to, and the cold street was not inviting, after the pleasant warmth and brightness of the church. He was a stray waif with neither father nor mother to care for him, and he picked up a scanty living by selling newspapers, eating and sleeping where he could.

That glimpse of the church had been almost like the opening of Paradise to Joe, and nearly every afternoon, at the same hour, he wandered there again. Sometimes his clothes were so ragged that he felt ashamed to go, but he tried to make himself clean, and, as the church was rather dark, he hoped that no one would see him. No one did see him, and no one missed him when he stopped going.

One afternoon toward spring a ragged-looking boy with a not very good face stopped Mr. Ainslie, the assistant clergyman, in the porch, as he was coming out after the five-o'clock service. It was very light now at five o'clock, and not at all cold, and Nick did not go into the church any more to warm himself.

" Please, sir," he said, half bashfully and half boldly, as he twisted his old cap around in his hand, " will you come and see Joe? He's sick, and he gets out of his head and sings things, and he talks about the church and would like a bit of it in his room."

" Well, my boy," replied the clergyman, kindly, " who *is* 'Joe'? And where does he live?"

Nick was astonished that a regular church-goer like Joe should be unknown to a person who might have seen him every day, but Mr. Ainslie finally gathered the information that Joe lived in Pleasant Alley—a region that the clergyman knew to be anything but pleasant— that he had once strayed into the church by accident and had been coming almost every day since, and that he was now supposed to be dying of a low fever.

" I will go to him at once," he said.

Mr. Ainslie felt pained to think that the child had gone in and out among that little flock of week-day worshipers without a word of welcome or encouragement, and he walked rapidly on under the guidance of Nick, who was only too happy to show him the way.

Kind people had cared for Joe in their poor way, and Mr. Ainslie found him in a clean bed with a tidy-looking woman bending over him. He was singing "Jerusalem the Golden," which he had caught quickly from the choristers, and Mr. Ainslie was struck by the peculiar richness and clearness of his voice.

"He does be talking, sir, of lambs and shepherds, and the like," said the woman, respectfully. "I think it's pictures he's seen, or dreams."

"Joe," said the clergyman, very gently, as the sick boy finished the hymn, "do you know that the Good Shepherd has sent me to seek for you, his little wandering lamb?"

"Has he?" exclaimed Joe, with a look of wonder in his eyes. "Oh, tell me about him!"

3

Mrs. Ricket, the woman in whose room Joe was, said she "never heard such a beautiful voice as that clergyman-gentleman had," and Joe too appeared to think so, for he lay perfectly quiet, listening to every word that he said; and all at once it seemed to dawn upon him that the Saviour really loved him and was calling him to himself.

"Will it be better than the church?" Joe asked, joyfully, as Mr. Ainslie was telling him of the heavenly glories. "And can I really stay there for ever? Oh, I am so glad to go!" and with these words upon his lips the little wanderer went home to his Father's house.

CHAPTER II.

A SLIGHT MISTAKE.

WHEN Miss Harson had finished "The Story of Joe," she was quite sure that she heard a sob or two on each side of her, and a sound very much like it seemed to come from the direction of the door that opened into the hall; the other door opened into the young lady's own room. The "hospital" was rather dark yet, on account of the children's eyes, and whoever was sobbing over there was not very plainly seen.

"This will not do, dears," said the governess; "I would not have told you the story had I thought you would cry over it, because that will keep you from soon getting well. And why should you cry, when little Joe was so very happy to go to the loving Saviour who has prepared such a beauti-

35

ful home for all who love and trust him?
Have you forgotten the hymn?—

> " ' I think, when I read that sweet story of old,
>   When Jesus was here among men,
> How he called little children as lambs to his fold :
>   I should like to have been with them then.' "

No, the children had not forgotten it,
and their tears were soon dried in repeating the beautiful verses with Miss Harson.

"What has become of Malcolm?" asked
Clara, suddenly, as though she had just remembered his existence ; for the little girl
had been too sick to think much of anything. "Has he had the measles too?"

"Not many," replied a very funny voice
from the distant corner, and presently Malcolm came into full view.

"Oh!" exclaimed the two voices together ; "how nice it is to see you again,
Malcolm! But you mustn't kiss us yet."

"I don't believe I could find a place to
kiss," said their brother as with more curi-
osity than admiration he surveyed the two
speckled faces.

"Of course not," laughed Clara, while

Edith was not at all sure she would not cry, "but we're going to be ever so pretty when we get well. Measles isn't becoming, you know."

"You're a dear little thing," exclaimed impulsive Malcolm, now rather ashamed of his speech, "and I wish I *could* kiss you. I've missed you and Edie ever so much. What made you go and have the measles?"

"Why didn't you have 'em?" was the reply.   .

"Jane said there wasn't enough of 'em to go round."

"There was, too," said Edie, quite indignantly, "for Clara and I had more than we wanted.—Didn't we, Clara?"

"That's nonsense," said Miss Harson, laughing. "You would have had just as much measles, Edith, if Malcolm too had had it. For it is not proper to call measles 'them,' but 'it,' just as we speak of any other disease."

"But there seems to be so many of measles," replied Clara; and she certainly looked, poor child! as though there were a great many just then.

"We will find something pleasanter to talk about," continued her governess, brightly, "and I am quite proud to have one well child to depend upon.—You must entertain us now, Malcolm, with some of your out-door doings. What about the sleighing?"

"It's just splendid!" said Malcolm, enthusiastically. "And my new sled goes down the hill there like—like the wind. But I wanted Clara and Edie to be there too."

"Do you think, Miss Harson," asked a very sorrowful voice, "that when we get well again there'll be any snow left?"

"Do I think that little girls who get sick in the middle of January are going to keep it up until the spring flowers open their eyes? Why, I wouldn't *believe* it of them! Think of all the trouble they'd make me!"

"Now Miss Harson has got her funny expression on," said Clara; "but I know she thinks we'll get well pretty soon."

"I hope so, darling," was the affectionate reply. "And now it is time for a good long nap, after all this talking. I dare say that when you wake again the sun will be say-ing 'Good-bye' till to-morrow."

Edie woke first from her nap, and found that twilight was coming on. The fire cast pretty shadows through the room and made everything look different from what it did in the daytime. The snow was beautiful from the windows, and the sunset was red; the little girl thought it seemed just like Christmas-time. The rows of dolls' beds were as funny as ever, and reminded her that Miss Harson had made the room into a hospital ward. Jane was rocking very quietly in a low chair by the fire, waiting for the children to wake, but no one else was to be seen. Clara slept soundly, and presently Edith said in a low tone,

"Jane, isn't it pleasant here?"

"'Deed it is," replied Jane, going to the bedside, "if a body's got to be sick; but I'd like to see you around and well again, Miss Edith."

"Have you ever been real sick, Jane," continued the little girl—"as sick as I am?"

"Well, no," was the reply; "not to say as sick as that. I don't believe I've had anything as bad as the measles."

"Maybe you'll have something worse," continued Edith, in a solemn tone; "you might have small-pox, you know."

"Dear me!" exclaimed Jane, in dismay. "What makes you say such things? It just makes my flesh creep."

"Does it really creep?" asked the little invalid, sitting right up in bed in her excitement. "Can you see it crawling? And where does it go to?"

"What's 'crawling'?" shrieked Clara, who found herself suddenly awake. "Don't let it come over here!—Oh, Miss Harson, Miss Harson, please come and take it away!"

Poor Jane was very much bewildered at the turn which things had suddenly taken, when everything seemed so peaceful, and, not knowing what else to do, she rang the bell violently. This brought every one to the rescue, and it was a relief to find that nothing dreadful had happened; but it took some time to quiet Clara and persuade her

that Edith had not been speaking of insects
of any kind. Their talks about "flyers and
crawlers" seemed quite forgotten, but she
was still a sick, weak little girl; and when
Dr. Gates came in soon after—as he fortu-
nately did—he gave her something soothing and said that for two or three days
there must be no more stories and exciting
talks. So Malcolm was banished from the
hospital, but, as he was a boy and had a
sled, he managed to live through it.

CHAPTER III.

THINGS were going on finely in the Elmridge hospital, and Clara and Edith even had their little blue wrappers on and were allowed to sit up for an hour or two every day. Kitty now had to make so much cream-toast and other good things that she declared the children were trying to make up for all the meals they had lost, but she always looked delighted when the tray came down empty.

Malcolm behaved so nicely, and was so subdued in voice and manner, that he was admitted to the ward every day, and he often showed a very pleasing interest in the symptoms of the sick dolls. Edith was not so grateful as he seemed to expect her to be when he painted Rosaletta's face with blotches, in imitation of her young mamma's, but Miss Harson soon made that

42

all right, and punished the mischievous
boy with banishment from the ward for
a whole day. This was all the harder because stories were allowed now, and Malcolm did not like to miss the stories.

" Here is a picture of the Children's Ward
in the hospital," said Miss Harson. " Does
it not look just like it—all except the pretty
coloring ?"

A very good photograph had been taken,
and the little Kyles were delighted with it.
It was in a paper called *The Heart's-Ease*,
published at the hospital every month to
tell people about the sick children there,
and Miss Harson often read to her charges
from this paper.

"Shut your eyes now," said she, when they
had looked at the picture, "and see if you
cannot imagine yourselves right in the ward
while I read you a description of it and of
the children who are there."

The invalids' eyes were obediently closed
when the governess, skipping the other part
of the description, began :

"'The corridor ends in the hall of the
Children's Ward, where texts are on the

walls, and over a contribution-box waves a pretty blue banner with this inscription : "For the Love of Christ and in His Name." The large, airy room has six great windows, through which it is flooded with sunshine. A strip of delicate blue carpet extends from the head of the room to the door. Eleven snowy cots with blue frames are ranged around the room ; eleven little wicker-chairs run with blue ribbon ; eleven picture-books are fastened to the cots ; eleven little towels with blue bordering cover eleven little tables at the sides of the cots.' "

"Oh!" said Edith, admiringly; "isn't it funny to have just eleven of everything?"

"Why, no, dear," replied Miss Harson, smiling; "it is not particularly funny, when there are just eleven children," and continued :

"'A large bath-room and lavatory are next to the ward. In the dining-room are three tables of different sizes; one is very low and, with its white tablecloth, tiny dishes and little chairs, has the appearance of preparation for a dolls' tea-party, but it is really for the accommodation of the wee bairns who may be able to go about. The pretty china is blue. Pictures are on the walls. A copy of *From the Manger to the Cross* tells these little ones daily, through its pictures and verses, the "sweet story of old" of the life upon earth of the holy Child Jesus. The two large windows are filled with plants; above them birds sing contentedly in their gilded cages. On one side stands a large baby-house completely and elegantly furnished, from bedroom to laundry; at the request of the former owner, it was given, after her death, to the Children's Ward. Near the door is a neatly-framed blackboard resting on an easel; it is the gift of an ever-generous, thoughtful friend. Another kind lady comes twice a week to teach the little ones how to use the blackboard, and also sends, every Sunday, pudding for the children's dinner.

" 'At present the ward is well filled. The cot not far from the door is occupied by "Little Grandma;" she is a wee mite of humanity and has the hip-disease, which compels her to use crutches. She is very much beloved and respected by her companions in suffering, and in return seems to feel for them quite a grandmotherly regard, and watches over them with the solicitude of more ancient grandmas. The little ones who have the use of their hands and feet delight to assist her to dress and undress, folding up her clothes and putting them neatly away. This little girl's father died when she was about six years old; her stepmother went off and left her with two other children, alone in the house. Some friends took care of the others, but for this poor little sick one no home could be found; so the good clergyman of the place sent her down to the hospital, where he knew she would receive the best medical attention, with tender care. She is now about nine years old, and under the skillful treatment of physicians and the loving thought and care of the nurses she has wonderfully improved.

"'Another cot is occupied by "Little Brown-Eyes"—a sweet little girl with beautiful brown eyes, clear skin, dainty little hands and pretty, well-bred manners which seem to indicate that some gentle blood flows in her veins. She suffers a great deal from terrible abscesses that break out on different parts of her body. Little Brown-Eyes has no father and is worse than motherless, for her mother leads a life of sin and misery, an unresisting victim of intemperance. Upon one occasion the wretched woman called, in a state of intoxication, to see her little child. She was told that she could not see her, for they would not let the little girl know that her mother was in such a shocking condition. After asking if the child was well the poor woman went off contented.

"'Then there is the "Little Mother." She came to the hospital " long, long ago " very sick, but now she is well and strong, and has passed from the ranks of the helped to the ranks of the helpers, and is a great comfort to those in charge of the ward. She mends all the clothes, sorts them out for the wash, and puts them away ready for use when they are brought from the laundry, besides fulfilling other responsible duties with great faithfulness.

"'A kind friend dressed some lovely baby-dollies for the children and gave them each one. No little children in luxurious homes are more ready to help others than these little ones. On Christmas eve one of the good women in charge went into the ward after the children were all in bed, and said, " Who will give me a doll for a poor little girl without one ?"—" I will !"—"I will !" —"Take mine!"—"Take mine!" came from all parts of the room, in eager childish treble; which shows how well they understood the sweet lessons of unselfishness and kindness taught them by their kind friends at the House Beautiful, and that they in their turn wished to give pleasure to other little ones less happily cared for than they.

"'But what do you think they did on Christmas night? At evening, when the lady in charge visited her ward and found three of them still up, she naturally thought it time for such wee tots to be snuggled cozily in bed, but they all looked so mysteriously eager, and the Little Mother seemed so disappointed, that she let them

stay up still a little longer. Something
nice was going to happen, you may be
sure. Very soon everybody was invited
to come to the children's dining-room.
And what did they see? Why, the Little
Mother and another young friend had
gotten up, all by themselves, some pretty
tableaux. One end of the dining-room was
shut off by a white sheet, which served as a
curtain. Then Little Brown-Eyes was seen
dressed as " Red Riding-hood ;" then came
the three little girls who were called " The
Gleaners," and they sang some songs the
Little Mother had taught them. And
with this pleasant surprise the happy day
came to an end at last, and the children
were tucked away in their little beds, there
to sleep, and perhaps to dream of Merry
Christmas.' "

" Oh how lovely !" said the children, in
delight. " But that isn't all, Miss Harson ?
Please read us something about that dear
little Nellie."

" Here is a long and very beautiful letter
to the ' Pansies,' " continued their governess, "as those children who are helping

4

to endow the 'Heart's-ease Cot' are called
—so you are both Pansies—and, as there
is a great deal in it about Nellie, I will read
you part of it. You will certainly like the
verse at the beginning, because it might
have been written about to-day:

> " 'Outside, gently the snowflakes are steadily falling,
>   Covering the earth in a mantle of white,
> Each tiny crystal its mission performing,
>   Hiding the desolate fields from our sight,
> Beautiful snowflakes, so bright and so lovely,
> • Floating so gracefully down through the air,
> Silently, steadily, still they are falling,
>   Emblems of purity fitting and fair.' "

The snow was indeed coming down so
quietly and steadily that it made the invalids sleepy to watch it, but there seemed
to be a promise now of sleighrides when
they got well; so they turned cheerfully
to the fire again, and waited to hear about
Nellie.

" 'And while slowly fall the snowflakes no
cosier place for a visit can be found than
the bright, cheery Children's Ward. If the
Pansies, one and all, will shut their eyes
very, very tight, perchance they will be
able to see in a snug corner, next to the

handsome mantel, a little blue-framed, snowily-draped cot half surrounded by a pretty pictured screen, over it an engraving—a country scene—while attached to the frame is a large scrap-book, and at the foot its little blue-ribboned wicker chair. In it, my Pansies, rests dear, patient little Nellie, for whom you all need to work, as she occupies what is to be the " Heart's-ease Cot." Her eyes are large and lustrous and her cheeks often brilliant—not with the rosy hue of health, but with the hectic flush of disease. This dear child is just such a sufferer as the warmest friends of the hospital rejoice to see sheltered there.'

" Then the letter goes on to tell how little Nellie was carried over from New York, and how, when the good doctor saw her, he said there was no help for her except in a very severe operation. This 'was entirely successful, and it is owing to his skill and the kindly care of the gentle nurses that Nellie is still among the living.

" 'When this dear, patient little child asked how she could thank the doctor for all he had done for her, she was told to say just what she really felt. She raised her dark-gray eyes to his face and said in soft, low tones, " Doctor, I want to thank you so much for making me better." Nellie is still weak, and, though now wheeled into the dining-room for some of her meals, has to spend the most of her time in bed, and often says, with a little sigh, " I am so tired !" She has ever been the same patient little invalid—never fretful or cross, and always thoughtful for others. When asked by one of the doctors what she would like to have to eat, she said, " I will take just what you think is best for me." At another time, when suffering, " I feel pain, but I try to keep the tears back." In a sweet little note written to her mother Nellie expresses the wish to be with her, but yet her willingness to remain at the hospital until she is better.'

"And that, I think," concluded Miss Harson, "is enough of the Children's Ward for to-day."

"I do so like to hear about it," said Edith. "And that little Nellie is just a darling. I wish I could be good like that."

"I wish I could too!" said Clara. "Let's try ever so hard, Edie. But I feel so cross when I'm sick."

"Pray, then, for a gentle, patient spirit," whispered her governess. "Perhaps this sickness is sent to help you to overcome this very fault, and to teach you to be patient."

Each of the little girls had tightly grasped one of Miss Harson's hands, and both were looking up at her with loving eyes, when Jane appeared with the tea-tray, which looked so very different from common that for a moment they wondered what could be the reason. It did not take them long, though, to find out. Jane came very soberly up to the little table on which they took their meals, trying to look as though everything was just the same as usual; but no sooner had the tray reached the level of their astonished eyes than the children fairly screamed with delight. There was a beautiful set of blue-and-gilt china for two—two plates, two cups and saucers, two

of everything, and such a lovely little tea-
pot, sugar-bowl and cream-jug. There was
a nice white card, on which was written,
"With papa's compliments."

"Just as if we were grown ladies," said
Clara.

"Oh! *Oh!*" exclaimed Edie, in a perfect fever of delight; "I just want to
eat it!"

"The card or the china?" asked Malcolm, who had been wonderfully quiet for
a long while.

Miss Harson thought it time to raise
the cover of a pretty little tureen that
held some stewed oysters all smoking hot
—just six apiece; and, besides this, there
were a slice of bread for each, some nice
little cakes and cambric tea. For the
invalids had stopped living on air, and
were hurrying with all their might to get
well.

"I'm so glad it's blue," said Clara as
she gazed affectionately at her cup and
saucer; "it's just like the children's dining-room now. How nice it was in papa
to think of it!"

The governess smiled, but she did not think it necessary to say that *she* had asked Mr. Kyle to buy a blue *tête-à-tête* set for the occupants of the sick-room.

CHAPTER IV.

SUNBEAMS.—A FUNNY DREAM.

D R. GATES said that the little Kyles were getting on famously, considering what a very greedy slice of measles they had helped themselves to, and they could now enjoy their meals and have the curtains raised enough to see what was going on outside. Malcolm obligingly made a snow-man in full view of the sidewindow and never forgot to bow and to smile whenever he passed, but for a long time one day seemed to go on very much like another, and the invalids were still unable to read or to do much toward amusing themselves. If, as Clara said, it had not been for that hospital of dolls, they would not have known what to do; but she was very thankful to have them all sick. One was named " Nellie," and another " Little Brown-Eyes," another " Little Grandma,"

56

and so on through the names of all the children they had heard of as being at the hospital. Sometimes the little sisters took it into their heads to cry over these sick infants—just as they supposed they might be doing if they were real children ; but their governess told them that crying was rarely known in that sweet and peaceful Children's Ward.

"Will not you read us what you wrote about the Sunbeam Cot, Miss Harson?" asked Clara, who was also mouthpiece for Edith.

"Yes, dear," was the reply, "if you are not tired of it, having heard it two or three times already."

Being assured by the children that they could not be tired of it if they heard it every day, the young lady felt sufficiently encouraged to give them another reading of the Sunbeam Cot:

"'Is not this a beautiful name for a hospital bed? And a "sunbeam" indeed was the young life—now ended *here*—in loving memory of whom the cot has been endowed.

"'Elizabeth M. B—— was taken a few months since from a beautiful home and loving parents, after a short sojourn of nine years on earth, to that "happy land"

> "'" Where loyal hearts and true
> Stand ever in the light,
> All rapture through and through,
> In God's most holy sight."

So sweet and sunshiny had been those few bright years cradled in love and strewn with flowers that when she was stricken down with fever, and scarcely conscious of the loving, grief-stricken hearts around her bedside, those to whom she was most dear kept back their tears that she might pass directly from the sunshine of her earthly home to that of Paradise. There the *"Talitha cumi"*—"Little darling, I say unto thee, Arise!"—of the blessed One awaited her.

"'The sick-room was full of peace and pleasantness, for flowers and all beautiful things surrounded her who had been a very sunbeam to those aching hearts, and sweetly and gently the child-life ended its earthly mission, and the precious dust was laid to rest until the dawn of the world's great Easter day. "Asleep in Christ" is the inscription on a tomb in the Roman Catacombs, and of none could these words be more truly said than of the dear child who went smilingly to God, leaving an empty void in the desolated home.

"'The sunshine had gone with the household sunbeam, and clouds and darkness were round about, yet even out of this gloom there arose a voice of comfort that whispered of the divine love and of the multitudes of sick and suffering children who drag out their weary days as best they may in their comfortless homes. What could be a more appropriate memorial of a loved and loving child whose own sick-bed had been made sweet and beautiful with all that love and wealth could procure than to provide for some less favored little one a place where pain and sickness could be robbed of half their sting? So the Sunbeam Cot was endowed—that is, enough money was paid into the hospital treasury to support some sick child there always. A sunbeam indeed to sick children is the memory of little Lizzie, who, being dead, yet speaketh, and whose gentle spirit may perhaps hover lovingly about the cot which owes its name and endowment to her sweet life and early death.' "

" Oh, Miss Harson," said Clara, with a shaky voice, while Edith was weeping quietly, as she always did over the story of the Sunbeam Cot, " how *can* you write such lovely things ? And it's every word of it true, isn't it ?"

" Yes, dear, it is all true ; and the pretty cot with Little Brown-Eyes lying in it is there to tell the story over again."

" I am glad Little Brown-Eyes has got it," said Edie ; " it seems nice to have her there."

Edith did not explain why, but Miss Harson thought she understood, and to her too it seemed " nice."

" I wish we could have a Sunbeam Cot," continued Clara. " Couldn't we, Miss Harson ?"

" You can have two, dear," was the smiling reply. " Try to be real little sunbeams yourselves, even while you are in the hospi-

tal, always sweet and patient and thankful
for what is done for you, pleasant-spoken
to Jane, and as cheerful as aches and
weariness will permit."

"Like that dear little Nellie, who only
said she was 'so tired'? We've been ever
so naughty since we heard about her, but
we'll begin to be good again.—Will we not,
Edie?" .

The little girl would have said "Yes"
to anything that Clara proposed, but the
sisters were both really in earnest in trying
to become good and patient. When Clara
felt cross, a glance at the beautiful text
opposite her, "God is Love," kept down
the bad feelings ; and when Edie looked
at the Good Shepherd with the little lamb
in his arms, for very shame she stopped
fretting and crying. For had not Miss
Harson told her that she and Clara were
God's little lambs, and that he was watching over and taking care of them as much
as if they were really in his arms?

The children had a long nap that afternoon, and the dusk crept stealthily on until

there was no light in the "ward" but that
of the fire and the reflected light of the
white snow outside. It was very quiet in
the large room—no sound but Edie's regular breathing, for she was still roaming in
the land of dreams. Miss Harson was
lying down with a headache, and Jane
had gone on an errand some distance off
and had been delayed.

Clara did not mind being alone for a little
while, although she would have minded it
very much some time ago; but she tried
so hard to overcome her faults that it
really seemed to be getting easier. She
was now thinking of what Miss Harson had
told them about the Sunbeam Cot and wondering if she ever could be a real sunbeam,
when she became aware that there was a
sound of voices in the room. Very soft
and low it seemed, but the sound was
there; and presently she knew that her
beautiful Isabel, close beside her, was talking to Rosaletta, on the other side of
Edith's bed.

"What do you think of all this?" Isabel
was saying, with a somewhat grand air.

"Do you like being in the hospital? I never was in such a place before."

"I like it pretty well," replied Rosaletta, who was a very conscientious doll; "I like being anywhere with Miss Edith."

"That's more than *I* do, then, with Miss Clara," piped out Sarah Jane, a large rag doll with no expression in her face. "The way she used to bang my poor old bones about is just too dreadful to think of."

Now, Sarah Jane had not any bones, but as long as she thought she had it amounted to the same thing. She was a very battered-looking object, and Clara felt a twinge of conscience at her words, for she remembered how very badly she had used Sarah Jane just because she could be flung about without getting broken. She had scarcely seen the ancient doll for two or three years, and she said to herself, by way of excuse, "I was little then."

"It does my poor old limbs good to lie here in peace," said a very dilapidated creature in a pink wrapper which had once been a beauty, "though, if you'll believe me, I haven't many limbs now, so to speak."

"Where are they?" asked Isabel and Rosaletta, in one breath.

"How can *I* tell?" was the reply. "Careless children have broken them off, till I may say that I haven't a leg left to stand on. And my eyes used to open and shut so beautifully, but now they stare wildly all the time, so that I can't get a wink of sleep. I believe I'm going crazy."

"A while ago I heard a story," said a very comfortable-looking doll, "that I guess would frighten some young people we know. In this story the dolls were very badly treated by a little girl who pulled them around by their hair, and roasted them in front of the fire, and left them out of doors all night, and stuffed them into places that were too small for them, and did almost every dreadful thing to them that could be thought of. But one night they all came to life, and their little mistress herself turned into a doll; so they took her in hand and punished her well, doing the very same things to her until she was almost killed."

Clara shuddered. The talking sounded

very much as though these dolls had come
to life; and if they had, there were certainly dreadful things in store for her.

"I don't think it's nice to be revengeful,"
remarked Rosaletta, who had always been
treated with the utmost tenderness. "And
perhaps," she suggested to the doll who had
lost her limbs, "your legs and arms came
off very easily."

Beauty, as this doll had been called,
tossed her head at this, and said that she
"guessed her limbs were as good as any-
body's, any day;" and then she sulked and
would not say another word.

"Dolls have a pretty hard time," piped a
little voice from one of the farther beds,
"but what I mind more than anything is
the bath. If I were only wax with real
hair, Miss Edith would take good care not
to put me into water."

"I shouldn't like to be a china doll," said
queenly Isabel, with a superior air; "they're
so very small and—and—."

"Insignificant," added the little voice—
"although such big words nearly choke me.
Well, I didn't make myself, you see, but, as

5

I am made in this shape, I want to be just the best china doll I know how to be."

All the other dolls except Beauty applauded this sentiment, and the good-natured, fat little doll, who seldom had any clothes, was looked upon with respect.

"I wonder how long this being so dreadfully good is going to last?" said a frivolous damsel with golden curls. "Do you suppose they'll ever really do anything to help others?"

"Yes," replied Rosaletta, promptly; "I am sure that my dear little mamma will, and I think I can answer for Miss Clara too. They're just crazy to get well enough to go to work."

"Well," said a voice that had not yet been heard, "they'd better not try too much at once, or there'll be a breakdown. These are sensible lines to remember:

> "'One step, and then another,
>   And the longest walk is ended;
> One stitch, and then another,
>   And the largest rent is mended;
> One brick upon another,
>   And the highest wall is made;
> One flake upon another,
>   And the deepest snow is laid.

" ' Then do not look disheartened
    On the work you have to do,
And say that such a mighty task
    You never can get through ;
But just endeavor, day by day,
    Another point to gain,
And soon the mountain which you feared
    Will prove to be a plain.' "

Sensible as the lines were, Clara burst out laughing; for all of a sudden the comicality of dolls talking in this fashion and repeating poetry came to her so strongly that she lay there shaking with laughter and wondering if such a thing had ever been known before. But presently Miss Harson and Jane were standing beside her, while Edie gazed at her with frightened eyes.

As Miss Harson's headache had much abated, she was feeling better, and she was smiling down at her little pupil.

"What is it, dear?" she asked, affectionately. "What amuses you so?"

"I'm 'most sorry you came," replied Clara, rather wildly; "it was so very funny to hear 'em talk, and now they're as quiet as ever." She glanced at the two rows of dolls, who all looked as though they never had spoken a word and never meant to speak one.

"You dreamed it, dear," said the governess, smoothing back Clara's hair caressingly. "When people are not well, they sometimes have strange fancies of this kind."

But Clara insisted that she was wide awake; the whole thing seemed so real that she was not willing to believe it a dream.

CHAPTER V.

DELIGHTFUL surprises seemed to be constantly hiding in all sorts of odd places, ready to burst out upon the little patients at any moment; and Miss Harson said laughingly that the invalids were always expecting to be surprised. No children could come and see them—no grown people, either, for that matter, for every one was afraid of taking the measles; and pleasant things were constantly planned to brighten the long confinement within-doors. The hospital itself was a continual delight, and those dolls were always having new diseases; while, as to stories, Miss Harson said that she "had to tell so many she was afraid of forgetting how to tell the truth." The children wondered if there really was any danger of this kind, but they soon decided that

69

their governess, at least, was safe. Every
two or three days there was a letter from
some one by mail. Sometimes it was from
papa, sometimes Miss Harson and sometimes Malcolm, but they were all very interesting, and often funny, and they were
written on very much ornamented paper
and tied with ribbons—"Just like valentines all the time," the children said—and
all these precious letters were put in a
box, and frequently taken out for a fresh
reading.

One day it seemed to be "raining cats."
For each of the invalids Miss Harson got
up a remarkable letter with a bordering of
cats and kittens all around the sheets of
paper, with one cat's head on each envelope just where the seal ought to be.
The young lady had carefully pasted on
all these pictures, and she felt quite repaid for her trouble by the children's enjoyment.

But this was not all. When Dr. Gates
made his visit in the afternoon, he took
out of his overcoat-pocket something soft
and squirming and laid it beside Clara;

then he dived into the other pocket and
dropped another something beside Edith.
The most delighted squeals greeted these
strange performances, for on each bed was
a most surprised-looking little Maltese kitten with its eyes just opened, and it was
now using them in staring with all its
might.

"Oh! oh! oh! You *darlings!*" exclaimed two voices, with accompanying
squeezes, until the doctor declared that
the "Society for the Prevention of Animals," as Clara designated it, would certainly call two small girls to account if it
should happen to see them.

"How very kind it was of you, doctor!
How did you ever come to think of it?"

"You see," was the good-natured reply,
"we were presented with five kittens lately,
and this seemed to be a good way of getting rid of two of them. Besides, I thought
that two little sick girls would enjoy some
live playthings."

The kittens were most thoroughly ap-
preciated, and the children seemed in danger of being too happy.

Then, at tea-time, on the tray there was a little form of orange jelly in the exact shape of a cat—some of Kitty's doings—while rolled up in each napkin was a small chocolate mouse. But that unfortunate cat, instead of being presented with her natural food, was herself eaten, and the chocolate mice were used to amuse the kittens.

Clara's pet was named "Rose," and Edith's "Daisy," and they were distinguished by a pink ribbon around Rose's neck and a blue one around Daisy's. The children declared that no one but Miss Harson would ever have thought of anything so nice; and although the kittens did not seem to appreciate their neck-ribbons, as they tried with might and main to scratch them off, the ribbons certainly improved their appearance very much.

"Everybody is so good to us!" murmured Edie, in great contentment, as with Daisy in her arms she sat for an hour in her blue-trimmed rocker.

"And I shouldn't wonder," added Clara, peeping smilingly around at her governess, "if Miss Harson were going to tell us a story this very minute ; that's just the way she looks."

"Is it, Miss Harson?" asked Malcolm, eagerly. "And is it one of your very own?"

"Yes," the young lady replied, laughingly ; "I really was thinking of it. How many do I tell you a day now, I wonder? Everybody is very good to you, as Edie says, and I am rather afraid of your being spoiled ; but the words reminded me of a boy who thought quite differently and of how he was cured. The story may help you to remember that you must try to be good not only when all treat you kindly, but when they do just the opposite. I will call the story

"HARRY'S LESSON.

"'I think that everybody's just hateful ! So there, now !' exclaimed a very red-faced little boy on whose long eyelashes some suspicious looking drops were glittering. 'Nobody wants to do anything for me, and I'll just go off and be a hermit.'

"'That wouldn't be much fun, Harry,'

said his uncle, with a comical smile; 'you wouldn't have any one to scold then.'

"At these words Harry looked rather ashamed, as he certainly did do a great deal of scolding for a small boy. His uncle had more influence over him than had any one else, he was always so gentle and patient, and yet bright and cheerful— 'funny,' as Harry expressed it. But he thoroughly understood boys, for he had once been a boy himself, and he did not forget this. His nephew declared that, although he *was* a clergyman, he was not a bit afraid of him.

"'I do not think the people in this house are so very bad,' continued Mr. Gregg: 'I really believe there are worse ones; and, on the whole, they seem to treat *me* pretty well.'

"'Of course they treat *you* well,' exclaimed Harry, 'because you are always so good yourself; but—'

"Here Harry found that his uncle was looking at him in such a very comical way that he could not go on. He had to laugh, too.

"'Poor mamma!' said Mr. Gregg, 'and poor Aunt Clara and sister Minnie! for I suppose *they* are the "hateful" people of whom you complain. But do you ever think, Harry, whether they enjoy having a noisy boy burst in upon them—mamma with a headache, perhaps, lying on the lounge, Aunt Clara busy with her painting, and sister Minnie intent upon her lesson—demanding all sorts of things at once, and slamming the doors and scolding furiously if they do not fly to get him what he wants? You cannot live happily with people, Harry, as I once heard a wise old man say, unless you learn to take them by the handle.'

"'"Take them by the handle"?' repeated Harry, in a bewildered way.

"'Yes,' continued his uncle, 'just as you would take a hot kettle or saucepan from the fire: seize it recklessly, and you are burned; but grasp it properly by the handle, and it is lifted very easily. A better rule is the golden rule of charity, or love —doing unto others as you would have them do unto you. Before we judge other

people we must put ourselves in their places
and try to feel as they do.'

"Harry began to think that he had been
a very impatient boy, and Mr. Gregg, looking kindly into the frank, open face, said,
with a smile,

"'You are my namesake, you know,
and really, Harry, you are wonderfully
like what I was at your age.'

"'Oh, uncle!' was the surprised exclamation, with one arm around the clergyman's neck. 'Did you ever get mad and
talk like me?'

"'I am sorry to say that I did, Harry;
and I must tell you how I was cured of it.
I owe it to a dear old man who was a sunbeam wherever he went, and you shall hear
all about it. You must imagine two little
boys coming home from school one winter
afternoon a great many years ago. I was
one of them, and I said to my companion,
Tom Haines,

"'"Tom, we are going to have a missionary at our house this afternoon; I expect he'll be there to tea."

"'"Ain't you afraid of him?" asked

Tom.' "Missionaries eat people, don't they?"

"'"What a silly you are!" I exclaimed, proud of my superior knowledge. "You're thinking of cannibals, I guess. I am afraid of the missionary, though, because he's so awful good. Our folks are talking about him all the time and telling me to be sure and behave well."

"'I could see that Tom didn't envy me, though our visitor wasn't a cannibal. He said "he guessed he'd be awful cross," and I rather dreaded that myself.

"'I peeped cautiously into the sitting-room, and there was a venerable-looking old man with snowy hair and beard and the loveliest smile, it seemed to me, that I had ever seen; it made me think of heaven. Aunt Celia said that Mr. C—— reminded her of the aged St. John, with his oft-repeated words, "Little children, let us love one another."

"'The dear old man at once called me to him and began to tell me of the many places and people he had seen; for he had lived among the heathen for forty years.

He had suffered much and had been very
ill treated at different times; but of this he
had nothing to say. Many close questions
were put to him by different members of
the family, but there seemed to be only
love in his heart toward all, and rejoicing
because of the spread of the gospel. I
listened spellbound; it appeared to me as
if I could have heard the dear old missionary talk for ever.

"'At length some one questioned Mr.
C—— about Patagonia. He had once
spent three months there when it was in
its worst state, and he was absolutely
obliged to leave on account of the hope-
lessness of the work and the danger he
was in.

"'"How could you stay so long among
those frightful savages?" asked my mother. "Didn't they treat you dreadfully?"

"'"Well," said the old man, kindly,
feeling that there really was not much to
be said for the Patagonians, "I rather
think they treated me about as well as
they knew how."

"'All laughed, because they could not

help it: this was such an unusual way of looking at the matter; but there were tears in their eyes, too, as they gazed reverently upon the aged saint. His words made an impression upon me that has never been forgotten. He did some missionary work that day of which he probably never knew, and I resolved to be a different boy from that time forth. Often, when I have felt mad at people, Harry, and angry words would rise to my lips, I seemed to hear the old missionary's gentle voice and his kind judgment of those heathen enemies, and the waves of passion would subside. There is nothing sweeter than love and gentleness in return for injuries—the lesson taught us by our Lord and Saviour.'

"Harry thanked his uncle for the story, and determined to imitate so lovely an example. He did not always succeed, but he persevered, and after a while such words as those with which this story opens were never heard from his lips."

"I like that," said Malcolm, approvingly,

"and I wish I could have seen the dear old man."

"Was he real, 'Miss Harson?" asked Clara.

"Yes, dear, and he said those very words. He could scarcely be persuaded that every one was not good to him, and all through life he scattered loving words and deeds wherever he went."

CHAPTER VI.

A SECOND CHRISTMAS.

"I 'D like to play it is Christmas again," said Edith, rather fretfully. "What does it always run away so fast for? It takes so long to come when we watch for it, and then just as soon as it's here it's gone."

"Yes," added Clara, "that's just the way it always is. Here's my dear, darling Isabel, and the lovely books papa gave me, and the pretty pocket-book from Miss Harson, and all the lots of other presents, but they don't look as they did on Christmas morning. Why doesn't it last longer, Miss Harson?"

"The real Christmas does," replied the governess; "those who take the great Gift of all—the blessed Saviour—into their hearts do not forget the Christmas teachings as soon as the Christmas bells have ceased to sound, and that is what I want my little girls to remember."

"Couldn't you tell us a Christmas story?" asked Edie. "That would make us remember, you know. And then we could 'most think it was Christmas back again."

Miss Harson laughingly called her "a special pleader," but Clara was quite as bad, and the young lady went to her room for one of the little hospital papers, the Christmas number of the *Heart's-Ease*, from which she read them a story translated from the German. It was called

THE CHRIST-CHILD.

There was once a poor couple who had a single child, and they loved the child very dearly and would have given him a great many pleasures and gratifications if they had not been so exceedingly poor.

One winter, as Christmas eve came round, the child stood at the window and looked longingly out into the street at the houses opposite, where he saw lights, and where the Christmas trees were being lighted up for the children. Then the father went out

to get something for the child, and in the
street he found a handsome gilded apple
which some one had lost from among the
ornaments of a Christmas tree. Then he
bought a roll for a penny, and a colored
wax taper for a small sum, for the poor man
had no more ; and when he came home, he
lighted the candle and gave the boy the roll
and the apple ; and the boy was very happy
and thought he was quite rich. When the
mother told him that she had saved a little
wood and would warm the room and he
should have a mug of warm milk in the
morning, he was overjoyed, and danced
and clapped his little hands with delight.
Accordingly, he laid his roll in the table-
drawer, in order to have it to eat with
his milk, and played with great pleasure
with his golden apple ; he did not want to
eat it, for it shone and glittered so beautifully.

The next morning, when the room was
warm and the boy had taken his roll and
milk, he saw a handsome but very pale little boy looking in through the dim window,
which was half covered with frost ; the little

stranger seemed very poor and looked very
cold. Our little friend was sorry for the
child out of doors, because he had to be
hungry and cold on Christmas day. He
laid away his roll, set down his mug of
milk, opened the door and called the
stranger in to warm himself by the stove ;
he also shared his roll and milk with him,
and at last said,

"Now that I have a guest to-day, I will
eat my handsome apple with him." So
saying, he divided the golden apple with
the strange child.

Finally the visitor went away with many
thanks and many wishes of happiness and
blessing for his little benefactor. But it did
not seem as if these wishes were to be ful-
filled, for the poor people fell into greater and
greater poverty and suffering. Very soon
the husband, and after him the wife, became
ill, and both were unable to do anything.
So they lived a whole year in hunger and
trial ; and when Christmas eve came round
again, the father had nothing with which to
buy a taper or a roll for the child, and there
was not a penny for warm milk, or even for

fuel with which to heat the room. But the child had been taught to pray, for his parents were pious and trusted in God. They comforted their son when he was cold and hungry, and told him that in due time God would come to their help, even if he did not relieve them at once. The child believed this, and prayed earnestly for relief from such poverty.

And now, when it was so cold and dark, the door suddenly opened and a clear light fell into the little room. This light came from the beautiful stranger-child, who had returned again. He did not now seem poor, but very rich; for he wore a white, shining dress and a bright light was round his head, and he carried a cross in his hand, and a glittering Christmas tree. And after him followed twelve aged, venerable, kindly-looking men with white beards. Each of them had a great sack on his shoulder, and they took these sacks off and placed them before the child.

The Christ-child—for it was he, with the twelve holy apostles—spoke to the astonished boy :

"Last year you shared your apple with me, and I took the seeds and planted them for you in the heavenly garden of paradise. A great tree has grown up from them and borne fruit a hundred-fold, and that I bring to thee;" and he set the tree before the poor child, its branches bending down under the weight of the most beautiful golden apples. "And last year you shared your roll with me, and I have taken as many kernels of wheat as there were in the roll and sowed them in the heavenly garden of paradise, and the seed sprang up and has borne fruit a thousand fold, which I bring to thee to-day in return."

Then the Christ-child took the cross, put it in the stove and lighted it with a taper from the Christmas tree, saying to the boy that it was the cross which he had borne, and which should now be taken from him.

The sacks were full of the finest flour, and the apples of the Christmas tree were pure gold. And so the boy and his parents finally became rich and very happy people.

"Were they happy because they were rich?" asked Clara.

"No, dear: being rich alone never makes people happy. But it certainly was happiness to these poor people to be relieved from cold and hunger, and to be restored to health. They are described as being 'good and pious' in the midst of suffering; so we may be quite sure that they did not trust to their riches for happiness."

"I think it is beautiful," said Edith. "But oh, Miss Harson, how I wish—how I *do* wish—that lovely Christ-child would come here, into this very room!"

Clara looked almost frightened, but her governess replied gently,

"And why, Edie? Why do you so earnestly wish that the Christ-child would appear?"

"Because I would love him so," sobbed the sensitive child. "I would give him everything I have, and I would beg him so, when he went away, to take me with him."

"Don't!" whispered Clara, in an awe-stricken tone; "I don't like to hear you talk so, Edie."

The two little sisters were folded in each other's arms, while Miss Harson read them some beautiful verses which, she said, seemed to have been written almost in answer to Edith's wish:

> " ' Oh to have dwelt in Bethlehem
>   When the star of the Lord shone bright,
> To have sheltered the holy wanderers
>   On that blessed Christmas night,
> To have kissed the tender, wayworn feet
>   Of the mother undefiled,
> And with reverent wonder and delight
>   To have tended the Holy Child!'

> " ' Hush! such a glory was not for thee,
>   But that care may still be thine,
> For are there not little ones still to aid
>   For the sake of the Child divine?
> Are there no wandering pilgrims now
>   To thy heart and home to take?
> Are there no mothers whose weary hearts
>   You can comfort for Jesus' sake?'

> " ' Oh to have knelt at Jesus' feet,
>   And have learnt his heavenly lore,
> To have listened the gentle lessons he taught
>   On mountain and sea and shore,
> While the rich and the mighty knew him not
>   To have meekly done his will!'
> ' Hush! for the worldly reject him, yet
>   You can serve and love him still.

Time cannot silence his mighty words,
    And, though ages have fled away,
His gentle accents of love divine
    Speak to your soul to-day.' "

"You do find such beautiful things to read to us, Miss Harson!" said Clara. "And will you not tell us, please, how we can do something like that?"

Clara's governess understood just what was meant, and after a moment's silence she asked,

"Would you really 'like to play it is Christmas again,' Edie?"

"Ever so much!" replied the little girl, eagerly. "Can we hang up our stockings to-night, and all?"

"Not just that, dear. How would you like, instead, to fill some other persons' stockings?"

This had not been Edith's plan, but, remembering the little boy and the Christ-child, she answered promptly:

"It would be nice, I think, Miss Harson; but where are the stockings?"

"In Poverty Row. That is, there are feet there that ought to have stockings upon

them, but I am afraid they are generally
bare."

"Poverty Row" consisted of ten or
twelve little wooden houses standing high
on a bank that overlooked the bay, with
a beautiful view in front of them, beyond
the dust-heaps and ash-barrels around the
doors. The tenants in this row were always very poor and constantly moving in
and out. Miss Harson had just heard of
a family named Purse, very destitute and
consisting of a mother and four children.
The oldest girl, who was only nine, was
sick with fever, and the poor things—who
had moved there just before Christmas
and could scarcely get necessary food—
found it dreary enough.

"Are they as poor, do you think, as that
little boy's father and mother in the story?"
asked Clara.

"It sounds very much like it," replied her
governess, "and I shall go and see them at
once. But I have thought of something
which you and Edie can do for a second
Christmas, and I think it will amuse you
at the same time that it benefits them. I

will have Jane collect all your toys and picture-books, and you shall select such as you are willing to part with. Then I will have a pot of glue ready, to heal all wounds and fractures, and a needle and thread, to sew up rents, until you will be really surprised to see how well broken things can be made to look."

The children were delighted with this idea, and Jane had her hands full for some time in carrying Noah's arks, boxes of cups and saucers, kitchens, stray animals, washtubs and picture-books to be examined and wondered over and played with afresh. The animals had lost limbs, and the cups and saucers were broken and the picture-books torn; but Miss Harson took them in hand one after another and did wonders with them.

It was great amusement to the little invalids to watch their governess at this new employment, and Malcolm's tools and glue were also a great help. The torn pictures were nicely pasted on linen, and sometimes a little paint and odds and ends of ribbon made a great improvement.

"What a lot of things Mrs. Purse's children will have!" said Edith as she gazed admiringly at the fast-growing pile.

"It seems funny," observed Clara, "that her name is 'Mrs. Purse,' when she is so very poor. Purses, you know, always make people think of money."

"But she is an empty Purse," replied Malcolm, quickly.

"I think there are five empty Purses," laughed his governess, "and we must fill them with something besides toys. Papa kindly sends a store of flour, sugar, tea, potatoes and meat; Kitty has baked a plain loaf-cake with a little icing, and a sprig of holly stuck in the top; Malcolm means somehow to give each of the children a bag of candy—"

"*I* know!" exclaimed each of the little sisters: "he's taking his Christmas money for it. Can't we too, Miss Harson?"

"Not for more candy, to make the children sick, but you can buy a dozen oranges, if you like, for the little girl who is parched with fever. There is plenty to do."

Clara and Edith were very much pleased

with the idea of getting oranges for little Jane, and this second Christmas was almost as pleasant as the first had been. They were rather disappointed to find that Miss Harson did not think it best to send all the toys and books they wished to give, but, as the young lady said, the little Purses would not have known what to do with so many all at once, and a few at a time would be much better for them. So a picture-book and a box of toys were selected for each child, and the other things were put away until they should hear of some other needy children. Warm dresses which Clara and Edith had outgrown were made up into a bundle, which also contained a thick shawl and some other necessaries for Mrs. Purse; then, as Poverty Row was about two miles from Elmridge, Thomas brought a wagon, into which everything was stored, while Miss Harson and Malcolm had a delightful walk there over the hard snow.

Mrs. Purse, a delicate-looking, overworked woman with a baby in her arms and a small child holding her dress, was delighted, though at first she expressed her happiness by sitting down and crying as hard as she could cry, while the children gazed at the young lady and the little boy in open-mouthed wonder. Thomas deposited his parcels wherever he found room, and then returned to his wagon and drove off, thinking that Miss Harson and Malcolm would not be able to stand it there very long. They did stand it, however, until the place had been made more comfortable and there was a good fire burning in the stove, for Thomas had brought a bushel of coal for use until a ton could be sent, and this and the provisions seemed, as Mrs. Purse said, more good luck at once than they had ever known before. Then she told her sad story—how her husband, who had worked in a lumber-yard in Brooklyn, had been suddenly killed, and some one advised them to move into the country, where living was cheaper and she might get plenty of washing to do because there were so few to do it. They seemed to have forgotten that there were also few to need to have washing done, but Miss Harson would not discourage the poor woman, who certainly had her hands too full just now to do any washing if there had been plenty of it to be done. Little Jane's hot brow felt better after the young lady had smoothed it a while; and when she had eaten part of a large juicy orange, her throat was not nearly so dry.

"No," Mrs. Purse said, in answer to the questions that were asked her; "the children didn't have a bit of Christmas, for they were cold and hungry all day" (how Clara and Edie grieved when they heard that!), "and, although she didn't mean to complain, it did somehow seem worse on that day than on any other."

Miss Harson quite agreed with her, and she whispered something to Malcolm, who went out and broke off some large sprays of hemlock, of which there were two or three trees growing quite near; and when this was brought into the house and tied together, it made quite a respectable-looking Christmas tree. It was propped up carefully in a corner on a wooden box, for it was meant to stay there a while and brighten the room. A piece of Tur-

key-red which had been brought for this
very purpose was wrapped around the
box, and then some tarletan bags filled
with candy, bright red apples and golden
oranges fastened to wires and bits of gilt
and silver tinsel were hung on the tree,
while the boxes of toys and the warm cloth-
ing were placed all around it.

Such happy children as these little Purses
were are seldom seen, and while they were
all engaged in admiring the tree Miss Harson said,

" This is a gift to you from the little people of Elmridge, who are too sick to come
out and see you enjoy it."

"And from the young lady of Elmridge,"
added Malcolm, smiling affectionately at his
governess ; " it is she who has taken all the
trouble."

" We all enjoyed doing it together," continued Miss Harson, "and we have put the
tree just where Janey can see it nicely without sitting up in bed."

Janey said she had never had anything
half so beautiful before to look at and she
thought she should get well now.   Malcolm

Christmas in Poverty Row.

Page 96.

could not help smiling when the little girl said this so seriously, for he had never heard of prescribing Christmas trees for fevers; but, on the whole, he behaved remarkably well, and on the way home Miss Harson told him that she was proud of him.

By degrees the little Purses got over their first wonder at the Christmas tree and began to discover that some of the things on it were meant to be eaten, but their pleasure in it lasted a long while, and Mrs. Purse declared that Janey took a start for the better from that very day.

The "Ohs!" and "Ahs!" of the little Kyles were frequent while Miss Harson and Malcolm told them of the great delight in Poverty Row, and for the twentieth time they wished that they could have been there to see.

"No matter, Edie," remarked Clara, with a wise air; "it was lovely of Miss Harson to think of our doing it, and we know that it made the poor children happy, whether we saw it or not. And we'll always have two Christmases now, shall we not?"

7

Edith was quite ready to agree to this, but Miss Harson laughingly asked them what they supposed papa would say to such a plan.

CHAPTER VII.

LESSONS OF PATIENCE.

IN spite of the charms of Rose and Daisy—who certainly were, as their little owners declared, "the very cunningest kittens that ever did live"—in spite of all the pleasant surprises and the hospital ward and Miss Hatson's constant stories, the invalids were growing impatient for something to do. Dr. Gates said that it would not answer for them to use their eyes yet, and "it was *so* tiresome to have to use other people's eyes all the time!"

"What if you had to use them always?" asked their governess; and this made the children very still, for they knew that she meant their being blind.

"Are there any blind children at the hospital?" asked Edie.

"Not now, I think," was the reply, "but once there was—a dear little blind girl

named Bella. She was the first occupant
of a pretty white crib tied with bows of
blue satin ribbon which stood in the centre
of the ward. One of the helpers, who loved
her very much, has written a short account
of her. She says:

"'About a year before Bella came to us
she was taken sick with water on the brain;
her mother was living at service in a family,
so she sent the dear child to the hospital to
be taken care of. The disease left her with
paralysis of the spine, so that she had to be
lifted out of bed, and it also left her blind.
I. think she was the happiest child I ever
saw. She almost always had a bright smile
on her face, so patient was she, and so
good.

"'Little Bella suffered very much with
her head; and when a spasm of pain passed
over her face, the nurse would say, "Bella,
do you feel badly, dear?" She would always answer, "No; only my head hurts me,
that's all." At one time a lady who was sitting by her bed and talking to her asked
the child what was the matter with her.
Little Bella answered, "Nothing much,

only my head hurts me, I can't use my limbs, and I am blind, that's all."—"Why, you dear child," said the lady, "I think that is enough." Then she added, "You are a very happy little girl; what makes you so happy?" Bella answered, "Because every one loves me; the nurses all love me, and Jesus loves me. Don't you think I ought to be happy?"'"

"What a dear little thing!" exclaimed the children.

"'Bella knew us all by our step. In the morning she would call each patient by name as she heard a sound from a bed, and would ask them all if they felt better. If any were not, she would say, "I feel very sorry for you."

"'When the dear nurse in charge of the ward went away on her vacation, the children in the ward were going to write a letter to her. Bella, hearing them talk about writing and what they were going to put in the letter, said, "Oh, I wish I could write a letter to Nurse, too!" She said to a young girl who occupied a bed near her, "Priscilla, will you write a letter for me if I tell you

what to say?"   So Bella dictated, and Priscilla wrote it.   In a short time the answer
came, but the happy spirits of both the
children were with the Saviour they so
dearly loved.

"'Bella was very fond of singing, and
those who visited the hospital at that time
may remember how sweetly she used to
sing.   She would say, "Would you like to
hear me sing 'There is a green hill far
away'?"   She used to think this hymn so
pretty.   She tried to sing it the day before
she died.   She began the first line, but was
too sick to finish it.   She said, "I can't sing
any more."   The next morning she went
home to paradise, to be for ever with her
Saviour.

"'Little blind Bella, in the midst of her
suffering, seemed ever to "serve the Lord
with gladness," and this happy little mem-
ber of the great army of those chosen by
the dear Lord to serve him by enduring
pain and sickness, "strong in his strength,"
taught all around her that truly

"'"The light of his countenance shineth so bright
That here, as in heaven, there need be no night."'"

"We're not going to complain any more, Miss Harson," said Clara, softly; "we will try to be like dear little Bella. How lovely that story of her was! but it was so short. Will you not tell us something else?"

The young lady took up some pretty embroidery that she was doing—for the children liked to see the bright-colored silks—and after a few moments' thought she said,

"I think I must tell you about Louise, a little sick girl who for some time could neither hear nor speak."

"Was she deaf and dumb?"

"That is what many people called her," was the reply, "but it is not right; for only animals are really dumb. To say that a person is *dumb* means that he does not possess the organs of speech, and this is true of no human being; but to say that he is a deaf-mute—which is the proper name for those who can neither hear nor speak—means that he is speechless only because he is deaf and has lost all sense of sound. If my two little girls here should by some misfortune lose their hearing, I am afraid that they would soon forget how to talk."

"Oh," exclaimed Edith, "wouldn't that be dreadful! And did this poor little Louie forget how to talk?"

"Yes. She had talked like other children until she was five years old; then she had scarlet-fever very badly, and it left her entirely deaf. She forgot how to form words, and could only make some queer disagreeable sounds when she tried to talk. Poor child! I felt so sorry for her."

"Was she really a *poor* child, Miss Harson?" asked Clara. "And where did you find her?"

"I really found her," replied her governess, "sprawled on a gravel-walk at a country-house, where she had just fallen and scraped the skin off her nose. She was very angry indeed, not only because she had hurt herself, but because she herself had fallen down, instead of the child whom she tried to push off the piazza."

"How naughty she must have been!" said Edith, very gravely. "And was she deaf and mute then?"

"Very nicely said, dear. Yes, she was deaf and mute, except for making the queer sounds I spoke of; and it was this very thing that had made her so angry. She was very irritable with other children because they could not understand her half of the time, and sometimes they were rude and unkind enough to laugh at her. There were a number of children at the boarding-house where I was staying that summer with some friends, and many of them were not at all well behaved. Louie's parents were rich—for she was not a *poor* child, Clara, except in the sense of being unfortunate—and, as she was always handsomely dressed and had plenty of costly playthings, the other little girls would flock around her. But when she got into a passion, her companions flew right and left; for Louie's passions were dreadful to witness. The more angry she got, the less could she make herself understood, and the day I picked her up she was fairly foaming at the mouth."

"Why, that sounds like a mad dog," exclaimed the little Kyles, in surprise.

"It is indeed more like an animal than like a human being. But poor little Louie had lost all control over herself and was fairly raving. The little girl whom she pushed had excited her anger, and then, when Louie scolded her in her queer way, she laughed and imitated her, until, now perfectly furious, the deaf-mute child tried to punish her, and so met with a fall herself.

"I raised little Louie from the ground and led her to a side-door which was near a bath-room; here I wiped the dirt and blood from her face, and, finding that a piece of plaster was needed, I took her up stairs to my own room and made her as comfortable as I could. Mr. and Mrs. Dallas had both gone to town for the day, and Louie seemed to have fallen entirely to my care.

"The poor child screamed and howled, partly from anger and partly from pain, for some time after I found her, but gradually she became more quiet, until even the sobbing ceased, and she dropped off to sleep on my bed while I was smoothing her hair. I looked at her as she lay there, and saw such a distorted, passion-drawn face, with a deep frown between the brows, and an ill-tempered mouth, with the traces of tears on lashes and cheeks, that my heart fairly ached for her. Nothing but unhappiness could be her portion unless the expression of that face was changed by divine love in the heart, and I prayed earnestly that I might find some way of helping poor sinful little Louie.

"When Mrs. Dallas returned, she came to my room in great excitement; for she had been told that Nellie Lewis had pushed Louie down and hurt her very much. Louie was then sitting beside me on the lounge with her hand in mine, and looking almost happy in spite of the plaster on her nose; for she had soon discovered that I could understand her quite well, and we were already friends. Mrs. Dallas kissed her little girl affectionately and looked very sad when she saw how she had hurt herself, but she was not surprised when I told her about it, and that the accident was really Louie's own fault. She sighed as she said,

"'If you only knew, Miss Harson, the responsibility that this child—who is my only one, and whom I dearly love—is to me! We have spoiled her, I am afraid, because of her illness—for she nearly died five years ago with scarlet-fever—and because of the affliction which followed it. We are constantly hoping that as she grows older and sees the disgrace of giving way to it she will learn to control this dreadful temper.—My poor little lammie!' as Louie nestled close to her; 'you suffer from it more than any one else does.'

"I could not help thinking, What if she had pushed Nellie Lewis off the piazza and hurt her seriously, perhaps even killed her? for had Nellie struck her temple, this might have happened. The idea was so dreadful that it made me shudder."

"I do hope, though," exclaimed Clara, excitedly, "that some one gave that horrid little Nellie Lewis a good shaking for treating poor Louie so badly and making her fall and hurt herself. She just deserved it."

"I didn't shake her, dear," replied her governess, with a smile, "but I talked that same afternoon to her, and to the other children, too, and told them how unkind and wicked it was to laugh at poor Louie, who was one of God's afflicted little ones, for whom he cared just as much as he cares for the brightest and happiest child among them. I reminded them of how much Louie was deprived of every day her life in not being able to hear or speak as they did, and how they could lighten her burden, and even help her to overcome her passionate temper, by being kind and patient with her."

"I knew that was the way you would do it, Miss Harson," said Clara, feeling rather ashamed of her "good-shaking" prescription.

"That is one of the ways of 'taking people by the handle' of which we were talking lately, and perhaps it really was a 'good shaking' morally, for children are apt to be unkind from thoughtlessness; and this little bevy took my talking in good part and promised to be careful for

the future. Louie, too, made constant
efforts to overcome her temper, and, although I often wished she could have
succeeded better than she did, there were
no more such outbreaks while we were
at L——.

"I felt very, very sorry for poor little
Louie in every way, and the child quite
clung to me during that month in the
country. Mrs. Dallas was a very lovely-
looking mamma; she had beautiful brown
eyes and hair, and her cheeks always reminded me of fresh peaches. She wore
such pretty dresses, too, covered with lace
and ribbon, and her little white hands
flashed and sparkled with jeweled rings.
I have seen Louie sit and look at her and
stroke her cheek or her hand, as though it
was a pleasure to touch anything so lovely,
and Mrs. Dallas would sometimes put aside
her novel for a moment and caress the child
affectionately. Then, again, she would say,
'Don't, dear; you tire me.' Louie always
understood this, and the frown between her
brows would deepen, while her mouth had a
sorrowful quiver."

"Perhaps her mamma was too pretty to be nice," said Edith, with great gravity.

"She was certainly very pretty," continued Miss Harson, "and very 'nice' too; but she was quite young, and she did not seem to realize about poor little Louie. She was gay and fond of dress, and she spent so much time in trying to be happy that she did not think about the only things that could really make her so."

"What kind of a papa had Louie?" asked Clara.

"He was a very kind, pleasant gentleman, not much older than his wife; and when he was not at his business in the city, he spent his time in playing croquet, smoking cigars and driving about the country. He seemed fond of Louie, and often had her on his knee; but it mortified him very much that she was not like the other children."

"I love to hear about Louie," said Edith. "When they went away from the country, did they go to live in the city?"

"Yes," replied her governess; "they had a beautiful home to go to, and it had been put in perfect order for them while they were away; and Mrs. Dallas used to tell me a great deal about the luxurious conveniences of this house, 'which was the most perfect home,' she said, 'that could possibly be imagined.' But these things, though very delightful, do not make a true home, and such a family as Mr. and Mrs. Dallas and Louie would scarcely make that anywhere. Louie cried and screamed when we parted—for she loved me—and could only be pacified by my promising to go and see her very soon in the city."

"I hope you don't love Louie very much?" whispered Clara, rather anxiously. "You are our own dear Miss Harson now, you know."

"Do not be jealous of Louie, dear," said the young lady, softly; "she is now, I hope and trust, with the Saviour to whom little Bella went so gladly. I did love her very much when she was here, both because I was so sorry for her and because she seemed to depend so much on me. But I must tell you of pleasanter things about this little girl now, and how she really learned to talk and how she became so bright and happy."

"Oh, could she?" exclaimed Edie. "I am so glad!"

"Yes. A kind physician who heard me speak of Louie and her affliction told me so much about an institution for deaf-mutes which he had visited that I went to Mrs. Dallas and asked her to send Louie to this school. At first she did not like the idea and said that she preferred keeping her afflicted daughter at home, but Mr. Dallas took up the matter warmly and urged his wife to give her consent. Louie herself was like some wild thing when she understood that she might be taught to speak, and fairly hung upon her mother, praying and beseeching her to let her go, until Mrs. Dallas consented.

"Beautiful garments of all kinds were prepared for Louie, and her handsomest doll and books, with a quantity of cakes and confectionery, were carefully packed in an elegant trunk. Little Miss Dallas went off in style, and her father and moth-

s

er went with her. This and the blaze of
excitement she was in at the idea of learning to talk like other people prevented her
from realizing that she was leaving home to
go and live among strangers. But love and
tenderness met the solitary child at the very
threshold, and it was not long before Louie
felt that her lines had indeed been cast in
pleasant places. The sight of so many
children affected in the same way prevented her from being embarrassed by the want
of speech, and these children all seemed
happy and hopeful. Some of them told
Louie that they were worse than she was
when they first came, and now they could
speak almost like other people. The kind
principal and the teachers were much beloved, and obedience from love, not from
fear, was the order of the school. Many
of the rules Louie did not like, and the
early rising-hour—half-past six—was a
great trial to her; but she found that
many girls only a little older than herself
rose at six, and she tried hard to overcome
her love of her bed in the morning. She
wrestled, too, with her violent temper, and

practiced keeping perfectly still when she was angry. Poor child! all this was hard work at first, but the school was a house of prayer, where one of the first things a pupil learned was that

"'The smile of the Lord is the feast of the soul,'

and that to do right is the best and highest aim.

"Louie was really happy at the institute and improving daily; but during the first winter of her stay she took a heavy cold that lasted two or three months. Finally she was sent home to get well. Her parents were delighted at the change in her. She had grown into a pretty and graceful child, and had almost forgotten how to frown. She could talk a little, too, although not very well as yet, and her love and gratitude to her teachers seemed unbounded. But her 'pretty mamma' was as fondly loved as ever, and Mrs. Dallas seemed to take pleasure in her caresses and had her little daughter with her constantly. Mr. Dallas, too, was no longer mortified by the bright little Louie who could understand nearly everything he said by watching the motions of his lips, and both papa and mamma were careful of the delicate child, whose cough was an obstinate one.

"With the smiling skies of May, Louie's health improved, and she ran and played through the long summer days with such keen enjoyment that it really seemed as though disease had been conquered. Her clear, sparkling eyes, rosy cheeks and smiling face made people pronounce her 'the picture of health,' and she returned to the institute in September, feeling, as she said, 'so strong and well.' Every one spoke of her improved looks, and especially of the fact that she was now so happily rid of her bad cough.

"In a month or two Louie's rosy cheeks faded and her step became more languid. The cough came back. She could not study much, and she might get up now at any hour when she felt like it. Finally, the sick child begged to be taken home, and on a bright morning in January her father came for her and wrapped her up carefully for the

journey. It seemed likely to be the last
one Louie would ever take. In her beautiful room at home everything had been
gathered that could possibly please her,
and for some time Louie was able to sit
up and enjoy all these pretty belongings.
But she suffered greatly, and that terrible
racking cough struck a chill to the hearts
of those who loved her. She was such a
changed Louie, for she would smile after
one of these paroxysms, and say, 'Perhaps
there will not be many more.'

"'You are suffering so, Louie!' I said
one day when I had gone to sit with her a
while. 'I cannot bear to see it.'

"'But, Miss Harson,' she replied, with a
surprised look, 'God wants Louie to suffer;
perhaps this is the only way I can go to
him.'

"'Then you would not be made well
again,' I asked her, 'unless you were quite
sure it was God's will?'

"'No, indeed!' said she, with so much
emphasis that I could not doubt her being
in earnest.

"But what a wonderful work had God

wrought in this once froward and most un-
lovely child, now full of faith and love toward her unseen Saviour and waiting
patiently for her release! This came in
April, when the first violets were peeping
above ground; and when little Louie was
laid to rest, Mr. and Mr. Dallas felt that
they had not loved their child half enough.
They built a beautiful home for poor children in memory of their little daughter,
and through her patient suffering and
Christian death they were both led to
the Saviour whom Louie loved."

The two little girls were very quiet after
this story, and Malcolm, who had come in
somewhere about the middle of it, whispered that they were asleep. But Miss
Harson knew better.

CHAPTER VIII.

SOME HOSPITAL-BOYS.

THE next day Malcolm began in a rather lordly way, as though he thought he had been too long overlooked:

"I think it would be nice to hear about some boys now, Miss Harson, we have had so many girls."

"And pray, sir," asked his governess, "what right have you to say 'we'? Are you in the hospital?"

"No, ma'am," with a humble bow, "except as a visitor; but I thought—"

"You have no right even to think, where you are allowed only on sufferance. But I will take the vote of the ward and see what is to be done with you."

"The ward," however, only giggled rather unmeaningly; and when the young

lady continued, "Shall we grant this in-
truder's request and have something about
boys?" it merely said, "Yes, if you please."

"Isn't there any boys' ward in St. John's
Hospital?" asked Malcolm.

"Certainly there is," was the reply, "but
it is smaller than the Children's Ward, and
not so often filled. Tiny boys are put into
the large room when there are unoccupied
beds for them. There are six white-draped
iron bedsteads in the Boys' Ward—three
on each side—and by the side of each bed
there are a rug, a chair and a small table.
A strip of bright carpet is laid through the
middle of the room, and the rest of the
floor is stained brown. A comfortable
rocking-chair stands here and there for
those who are able to sit up; near the
door there is a large set of hanging-
shelves for books, and these are well
filled with delightful reading. The wide
window-sills are full of flowering plants
and vines. Everything in this room was
given by a lady in memory of a beloved son
who was called to God in his early youth.
In this way the money that would have

been spent on him has for his dear sake thus been devoted for the good of others."

"I like to hear about the Boys' Ward, Miss Harson," said Clara. "Is there anything more?"

"Just opposite the door, in the hall, there is a handsome screen in rich colors, with these inscriptions:

In Memory of

WILLIE LEWIS, 1881.

GOD SHALL WIPE AWAY
ALL TEARS FROM THEIR EYES.

HE GIVETH HIS BELOVED SLEEP.

HE HEALETH THE BROKEN IN HEART,
AND BINDETH UP THEIR WOUNDS.

SAVE US, O LORD, WATCHING;
GUARD US, SLEEPING.

This screen was presented by a Sunday-school in memory of a lovely boy of sixteen whose short earthly life was ended at the hospital. Another boy-patient carved the pretty contribution-box which is fastened on the wall near the screen, and the blue banner over it has this motto:

FOR THE LOVE OF CHRIST,
AND IN HIS NAME.

Sometimes the boys who belong in this ward are able to be out of it doing some light work, and I have never seen the sick-beds all filled at once. Perhaps," added Miss Harson, "you will not object to another account of such a ward, which I have written in the shape of a story?"

A general laugh was the only answer, except Edie's declaration that "Miss Harson was just too funny for anything!" and so the story was told. It was called

MINNIE'S HOSPITAL-WORK.

"Cousin May," said Minnie Fane, "I don't see how such a little girl as I am could do any good to the sick people at the hospital, but I'd like to go there with you, if you wish to have me."

"Every one who is willing can do something," was the reply, "and when you have

been there you can tell better what that
something is; so, if mamma is willing, we
will start for the hospital."

"Yes, indeed!" laughed Mrs. Fane;
"you are welcome to my troublesome
little daughter, if you want her." But
she gave the "troublesome little daughter" a very loving kiss, which Minnie returned with interest.

Cousin May was no cousin at all, but a
young lady who had a great many friends
among the little people as well as among
their mothers, and who spent a great deal of
her time in visiting the poor and the sick.
She was very successful, too, in getting
those who were better off to help them,
and there was always something even for
the children to do. But Minnie Fane—
who had lately been very proud of her
twelfth birthday, and who was very fond
of Cousin May—wondered what she could
possibly do in a hospital. She could carry
things, she said, if mamma would give them
to her; but Cousin May only laughed as
she told her that *she* would take all that
was needed.

"How very still it is!" said the little girl as they walked up the broad stairs and through the wide halls.

It *was* still, but it was sweet, too, with such great sunny windows filled with plants and vines as green and blooming as though it had been June instead of being January. Minnie thought that it was a wonderfully nice place to be sick in, if people must be sick at all.

Cousin May went directly to a ward that was smaller than the others, for it had only six beds in it, and four of the beds were empty. In each of the others there was a boy, one about Minnie's age, and the other a year or two older. The younger one had a round freckled face and hair that seemed to stick straight out, and the little visitor at once said to herself that "he wasn't pretty a bit." The other boy was thin and pale, with great, sad-looking brown eyes, and Minnie felt so sorry for him that she could have cried.

"Now," said Miss May, cheerily, "how are my boys to-day? I have brought a young lady to see you because I cannot stay with you long, and I think she can show you how to do something that will make the lying in bed seem easier.—This boy with freckles is Jimmie, and the one who looks all eyes is Harry."

The boys laughed as with a bright smile the lady introduced them, and they looked highly pleased with the visitor she had brought to see them; for Minnie was a pretty, pleasant-looking little girl daintily dressed in velvet and fur, and her hat had a long feather which in his own mind Jimmie compared to the tail of a kite.

"Here are some tools," said Cousin May, funnily, to her young companion, "and it will amuse the boys to see you work while you talk to them." She put a large crochet-needle and a ball of gray twine into Minnie's hands, and the next moment she was gone.

It was funny, to be sure, and not a bit like the way in which Minnie supposed people visited hospitals; but it was easy enough to do what she had already done so much of, for she dearly loved to crochet, and she set up a mantel-lambrequin at once.

It was so much easier than talking, and the two pairs of eyes were watching her movements with a great deal of interest.

Presently, Jimmie exclaimed, "*I* could do that; may I try?" and Minnie put the hook and twine in his hands. She thought it wonderful for a boy—and it would have been quick even for a girl to catch the idea so soon—when Jimmie managed, after one or two mistakes, to produce a very respectable "shell," and then he went on and made a whole row. He was delighted with the work and said that his broken leg did not hurt a bit now.

"Would you too like to do some?" asked the little girl, rather timidly, of the brown eyes that were gazing so wistfully at her.

"I don't believe I could," was the reply; "but if I had a pencil and some paper, I might make a picture, perhaps."

Away went Minnie to look for Cousin May, and she soon found her reading to a sick woman. The pencil and the paper and a thin, smooth book to draw on were placed beside Harry, and, looking almost as happy as his companion, he went to work at his picture. The young visitor wondered why he stared at her so much while he was drawing; but when he had finished, the reason became quite evident. He had made a very good portrait of Minnie, with hat and feather all complete, and underneath he wrote "A booful young laidy." So, you see, Harry's drawing was better than his spelling.

The boys declared that they had had "'most a *splendid* time" when Miss May came to claim her companion, and Minnie's face was as bright as possible.

Leaving Jimmie at his crocheting and Harry lying back, a little tired, gazing at his picture, the two hospital-visitors tripped homeward with the consciousness that they had been of some use to others.

" How did Jimmie break his leg, Cousin May ?" asked Minnie, with a very interested face.

"In saving the life of a little child that had crept almost under the horses' feet," was the reply ; " the wagon went over Jimmie's leg instead."

" Oh !" said the little girl, with a shudder.

"Wasn't that lovely of him? I am so glad he likes to crochet. Is Harry very sick?" she continued. "He looks so tired all the time."

"Yes, dear; he does not suffer much now,' but he will scarcely be any better. His drawing, though, will brighten many a weary hour, and perhaps, if you had not done your crocheting by Jimmie's bedside, no one would have found out that Harry likes to draw; so you see that even a little girl can do good to sick people."

·Minnie had many a pleasant visit to the Boys' Ward after this, for now she felt sure that she was wanted; and when other sick boys came there, Jimmie and Harry always claimed the "booful young laidy" as their own particular property.

"How delightful that was!" exclaimed Clara. "When Edie and I get well, Miss Harson, can't we go with you and teach some of the boys at St. John's Hospital to crochet?"

"First," replied her governess, smiling at this sudden proposition, "we must find out if the boys wish to learn; some of them would think it queer enough to be taught girls' work, and such boys as Jimmie are not often found. Just at present our little invalids must use all their energies to get well and strong; there is plenty of helpful work in the world waiting for them to be able to do it.—I hope, Malcolm," added the young lady, "that you feel satisfied, now that boys have received a fair share of attention, and that you liked the story?"

"Of course I liked the story, Miss Harson, ever so much," was the reply; "but, after all, there were girls in it, and they had more to say than the boys."

"Now, Malcolm," said Miss Harson, laughing, "if you were not the little gentleman that you are, I should call that a rude speech. I know, however, that you did not mean any rudeness, and therefore excuse the remark. But you will certainly find that girls are in most things, and that the things are all the better for having them."

"Doesn't he like to hear about girls?"

9

asked Edith, in surprise. "Why, I don't mind hearing about boys; I think they're both nice."

"So they are, dear," laughed her really good-tempered brother, "and you're just the nicest of them all."

CHAPTER IX.

VALENTINES.

THE winter was rapidly passing away, and Mr. Kyle said that there would not be much more cold weather; but this was not good news to the little invalids, who had not yet been out for a sleighride. They could sometimes stand at the window now and watch the sleighs as they passed, but they were not well enough to be exposed to the cold air. They could use their eyes a little, and it was about the twelfth of February when Miss Harson quite gravely asked if any of the hospital patients would like to send letters to their friends.

Clara and Edith scarcely knew what to say to this; but when their governess added, "Thursday will be the fourteenth of February—St. Valentine's day," they saw it all in a minute.

"Oh, Miss Harson," cried Clara, eagerly, "can I send one to papa?"

"Me too?" chimed in Edie, just as she used to do when she was quite a baby-girl.

"I think it will be a very pleasant thing to do," was the reply; "and now we will all sit at this large table, which Jane has moved in from my room—for I am not in a hospital ward, you know—and see what we can find in this parcel to make use of."

When the string was untied, there came to view a number of beautifully embossed and ornamented sheets of paper, with envelopes to match; some were large and some were small, but all were beautiful. This was one of Miss Harson's loving devices to amuse the little patients, and it succeeded admirably. They were very much surprised and delighted as these treasures were unfolded, and they could scarcely decide which was handsome enough for papa. At length a beautiful bird in a gold cage—the cage being made of gilt paper cut like lattice-work and lifted by a blue silk tassel—was settled upon, and, being requested to do so, Miss Harson wrote on the other page, "From your loving little Clara and Edith."

"Oh," said Clara, with a distressed look, "I forgot: people mustn't know where valentines come from. If only we hadn't signed our names!"

"He would probably have guessed, dear," replied her governess, soothingly; "so I really don't think it matters."

"Besides," added Edie, with a wise look, "I want him to know, it's such a pretty one."

Edith rather wondered why Miss Harson and Clara laughed, but she was too happy not to join them, and presently the two little sisters were whispering together, having first asked their governess to excuse them.

Presently Clara said with flushed cheeks,

"Would you mind, Miss Harson, if Edie and I should each take out a valentine to keep? No, not to *keep*, exactly. But don't ask us about them now, please."

"You're going to know all about it," said

Edith, mysteriously, " and I don't think you will mind—"

Here Clara touched her sister very suddenly under the table, and Edith stopped in such a comical way that Miss Harson could scarcely keep from laughing. She knew exactly what the innocent little conspirators were planning, and she wished that she could help them ; but half of the pleasure was in her being surprised, and she answered kindly,

" They are all your own, darlings, to do with as you think best, and I shall ask no question whatever. I wish you to get all the enjoyment that you possibly can from these pretty sheets, and I am quite sure that it will not be selfish enjoyment."

Two very happy little faces smiled back at the young lady, and the business of selection and of writing addresses went on briskly. There seemed to be valentines enough for every one, and it was quite a fortunate circumstance that papa had taken Malcolm to town with him for the day, as it made the present employment much easier. Perhaps the two little girls had murmured

at first when their brother went off so triumphantly, leaving them in the hospital,
but the murmuring did not last, and now
they were enjoying themselves so much
that no thought of out-door pleasures disturbed their minds.

Of course Mrs. Purse must have a valentine, and each of the little Purses; and
Miss Harson was much amused at Clara's
selection of roses and buds with two
printed lines,

> "I love you, I love you! 'Tis all that I can say.
> I dream of you all night, and think of you all day,"

to be sent to the worthy woman whose
mind was bent on filling the mouths of
four hungry children. But the motive was
a kind one, and the little girl never knew
that there was anything funny in her sending such a valentine to Mrs. Purse.

Something more substantial was sent
at the same time to the little house in
Poverty Row; for although, through Miss
Harson's efforts, Mrs. Purse now had some
washing as well as plain sewing to do,
which she did very nicely, it took so much

to feed and clothe them all that she could not get along without some help. But the good woman was especially grateful for that absurd valentine. She seemed to look upon it in the light of a prescription, for she said it really had done her good. Nobody ever sent her a letter, and to think of getting one like that was enough to be happy on for a long while. So perhaps Clara had not done such a foolish thing, after all.

Malcolm received a very beautiful affair with many Cupids over it, and most of the flowers that grow; while Jane and Kitty, John and Thomas, were all remembered. Clara—very secretly, as she thought—laid aside a valentine for Edie; while Edie—just as secretly—selected one for Clara.

A delightful morning was spent in this way; and when the important-looking letters were all ready, Miss Harson sent them to the post-office that they might be brought from there in proper style. The children were full of excitement and anticipation, for every one was to be "so surprised," and they could scarcely talk of anything else.

After their simple dinner .Miss Harson sat down beside the two little blue-wrappered figures as she said,

"Now that Malcolm is away—for there is not a boy in it—I am going to tell you a story that I wrote once about valentines. The story is printed in a tiny book that belongs to 'The Little Pilgrim Series,' and I think you will enjoy it to-day, for I have called it

"SOME VALENTINES.

"'Well,' said a little girl as she sat by the warm stove with a book in her hand on a snowy February day, 'this picture looks as if the children in it were having a grand good time. It is called "St. Valentine's Day," and the postman is just going off down the street after leaving them a great pile of letters. I wish he would leave some here.'

"Mrs. Forsyth looked up from the dress she was making to see what her little daughter's face said. There was no pout or frown there, for Marion was a pleasant-tempered little girl; she was only looking with a great deal of interest at the picture.

"'Did you ever get a valentine, mother?' she asked, presently.

"'Yes,' replied Mrs. Forsyth, with a smile; 'I did—once.'

"'Oh!' said Marion, starting up from her seat; 'tell me about it, please. Who sent it? And what was it like?'

"'God sent it, dear,' said her mother, softly, 'and it was like a dear little baby.'

"'I know! I know!' exclaimed the little girl. 'It was me, and to-morrow's my birthday.'

"'Yes, Marion, you are my valentine— the only one I ever had; and every year I thank God afresh for sending it to me. It will be nine years to-morrow since my valentine came.'

"Two little arms were wound about the mother's neck now, and a soft, round cheek was pressed against hers. They loved each other very dearly, this mother and daughter, for they were all the world to each other. Marion could not remember her father, because he died when she was almost a baby. Her mother made dresses for the people in the village, to help pay for the quiet and pleasant home in which they lived, for they had very little money of their own.

"Mrs. Forsyth was up early the next morning, for she had a great deal to do; it was baking-day, and she had bread to make, besides finishing off the odds and ends of the week; and it was Marion's birthday into the bargain.

"'Now, daughter,' said she, when the breakfast-things had been cleared away, 'do you not think it would be nice to give the first half of the day to the business of pleasing others? I am very sure that would be pleasing to God, and a better way of keeping one's birthday could not be found.'

"'But how can I please others?' asked Marion. 'I haven't anything to give them.'

"'I will show you, dear,' was the cheerful reply; 'no one is so poor as not to have something to give. You did not expect to receive any valentines; how would you like to send some instead?'

"'Oh, mother! may I?' with a delighted jump. 'That would be ten times better than getting them.'

"'Of course you may,' replied Mrs. Forsyth, laughing at Marion's excitement;
'there is no law against it. And I am
going to show you how to make them. I
think we can do about six, with the other
things that I must attend to, and you shall
say to whom they are to be sent.'

"On the table there was a large paper
box with some plain note-paper and envelopes in it, some pretty little pictures of
flowers and birds and butterflies, some gilt
bordering and other things, and beside the
box stood a bottle of mucilage with a
brush.

"'Let *me* make one, please,' said Marion,
quite beside herself with delight; and she
went to work in great haste and pasted on
the sheet a bird upside down.

"Nothing could be done with it now, and
it was such a gorgeous-looking bird that
it seemed a pity to spoil it; but Mrs. Forsyth did not scold: she only gently took the
brush from her excited little daughter and
kindly said,

"'This style of work has to be done
slowly and carefully; we must first plan,

and then carry out the plan. Watch me, and you will learn.'

"Marion quickly caught the idea, and she and her mother sat working together for a whole delightful hour, until six pretty valentines were spread out on the table before them.

"'First,' said Marion as her mother sat ready to direct them, 'there is Miss Bliss, our teacher. She is away from home, you know, mother, and sometimes she looks so sad—just as if she had been crying. I want her to have the very prettiest one of all— or 'most the prettiest,' she added.

"'This moss-rose picture,' said Mrs. Forsyth, 'will be the very thing; and on the other side I will write some pretty verses to comfort her.'

"The verses were beautiful, Marion thought; and when the ornamented sheet of paper had been carefully put into the envelope and neatly directed to Miss Bliss, the little girl felt very happy indeed.

"'It is ever so much more fun than if I'd got it myself,' she said; and her mother fully agreed with her. 'Now, mother dear,' she continued, with a loving look in her face, 'you know how very homely little Ann Somers is, and how poorly she dresses; the other girls are not always kind to her, and sometimes they even make fun of her. Yesterday, when they were talking about valentines, she said that she wished she could get one, and they all laughed at her and told her she was too homely, and that if she did get one they guessed she would not like it much. They were whispering together afterward, and looking at her, and I'm afraid they're going to do something that isn't nice; so I want to send her one of these pretty valentines.'

"A lovely bunch of pansies, or heart's-ease, was pasted on another sheet of paper and a pretty gilt bordering put all around it; then on the other side Mrs. Forsyth wrote a verse about bringing heart's ease to others, and Marion declared that the valentine was a perfect beauty and just the thing for Ann.

"For a crippled boy who lived near them Mrs. Forsyth arranged a picture of a cater-pillar turning into a beautiful butterfly, with

lilies and roses all around it; and the verses
she wrote for this one were about heaven
and the glorious bodies we shall have there.
How pleased Johnnie was when he got it!
and how he cried over it before putting it
away between the leaves of his Bible!

"Then Marion made a valentine for her
dear friend Lucy White, and this had two
hearts joined together in a wreath of roses
and leaves. There was another and plainer
one for Sarah Fay, an old colored woman
who went out whitewashing; and, although
Mrs. Forsyth could not help smiling at the
idea of sending Sarah a valentine, she quite
approved of Marion's doing it.

"There was only one left, and who should
have this? It had on it a bunch of daisies
and violets, which were Mrs. Forsyth's
favorite flowers, and Marion had done it
all herself. She timidly asked if she might
keep it; and when, after a while, her mother went up stairs, there it was lying on her
bureau. Mrs. Forsyth was quite as much
surprised as if she had received a real valentine from some one else, and a great
deal more pleased; for it was her own

little daughter who had made it, and she had made it for her.

"The other valentines were sent safely, for Marion herself took them to the different houses and slipped them under the doors without being seen. Then she and her mother had a pleasant walk together and went home to a nice little tea. She found that the cake which had been made and baked without her seeing it had pink frosting on it, and that her mother had contrived to make it with a rose in the middle. This was a delightful surprise, and Marion did not believe that any birthday-cake had ever tasted so good before. She heard from all her valentines and of how much pleasure they gave to those who got them; and, on the whole, this was the very happiest birthday that Marion could remember."

"What a nice story that is!" said Edith, admiringly.

"Yes," added Clara, "and I like it so much because Miss Harson made it all up herself."

"That is the case with nearly all the

stories I now tell you, dear," replied her governess; "you are always warned beforehand when I am reading you a story written by some one else."

"What a lovely birthday Marion had!" continued Clara. "But wasn't it funny to send a valentine to that old colored woman?"

Miss Harson smiled as she thought of the flowery epistle in store for Mrs. Purse, but the children seemed to consider this quite a different thing. They, at least, were very happy over it.

10

CHAPTER X.

ANOTHER KIND OF LETTER.

"YOU dear, lovely papa!" exclaimed Clara and Edith Kyle on the morning of the fourteenth day of February; "you ought to have fifty thousand kisses. Such beautiful valentines! O-o-h!"

This prolonged exclamation was the result of trying to squeeze papa within an inch of his life, for each little girl had received a beautiful valentine—one with a wreath of pink rosebuds around it, and the other with a wreath of forget-me-nots. But this was not all: right in the centre of the rosebud wreath there was a sparkling little ruby ring, and in the forget-me-not wreath an equally pretty one of turquoise; and both valentines were in lovely boxes the color of the flowers. On the pink one was written, "Miss Clara Kyle;" on the blue one, "Miss Edith Kyle."

146

"And why do you think *I* sent them?" asked the much-tumbled gentleman who finally emerged from the recipients' hands.

"Because, papa," replied Clara, sagely, "there is no one else. I know that Miss Harson didn't, and Malcolm couldn't; so it must be you. How beautiful they are!"

"I gave each of my little daughters a ring," said Mr. Kyle, "because they have been good and patient in this tiresome sickness, and I wished them to have something to remind them of it when they are no longer children; I hear such a good account of you in every way from Miss Harson that it gives me a great deal of pleasure. And here is a little parcel to be handed to your kind governess when she comes up stairs."

The parcel contained a beautiful little watch in a velvet box, and on a slip of paper was written, "A valentine for dear Miss Harson from her grateful and loving little friends Clara and Edith."

The children were very much surprised, for they had never even seen it before; but it certainly was nice of papa to let them give it, and they were so glad that Miss Harson had a cunning little watch of her own. There were tears in her eyes as she bent down to kiss her young charges, but they knew that they were tears of pleasure, and that a smile would soon come shining through them.

"This is a reminder," said the young lady, presently, "as well as a beautiful gift; it seems to tick constantly, 'Improve the hours '—or, rather, the minutes; for if these are carefully watched, the hours are sure to be improved."

"And our rings mean something, too," said Clara, who liked to be praised; "papa told us so."

"Yes," replied Miss Harson, "I know what papa was thinking of, for I was in the secret, you see; and that meaning will always be a pleasant one. But a ring is supposed to express the solemn word 'eternity,' because it has neither beginning nor end. The circle also is used to represent 'Him who was, and is, and is to come;' that is why we so often see it among the designs on church windows. We will remember these things, dear children, but at the same time we can rejoice in our pretty gifts and smile back at this glorious sunshine which is streaming in through the windows like molten gold."

Jane said that "it was 'most an elegant day" and she "guessed winter's back-bone was broken."

"What does she mean, Miss Harson?" asked Edith, when the girl had left the room. She thought the remark had a dreadful sound, and, although she had not enjoyed winter while she was too sick to go skating and sleighriding, she did not quite like the idea of having its back-bone broken.

"She only means," replied her governess, with a smile at the little girl's puzzled face, "that the worst of the winter weather is over, and she may be right; but the fourteenth of February is rather early to count winter over in this latitude."

"It seems just like spring to-day," said Clara, "but I do hope it will snow again, for us to get one good sleighride."

"You are quite safe to count upon it, dear," said Miss Harson.

"Yes," added Malcolm, who had come in

a few minutes before; "the paper says we are to have ten more snow-storms yet, and papa says that the paper 'most always knows about it beforehand."

"'Ten'!" exclaimed Edie, in dismay, although she too had been wanting enough snow for just one sleighride. "Will—not —that—be—dreadful!"

"Not so very, dear," was the laughing reply; "they will not all come at once, and some of them will probably be very slight— what are called 'flurries.' But our business just now is to enjoy this delightful day, and not to be looking for trouble ahead.—What have you there, Malcolm? Letters for any of us?"

"Yes, ma'am; I should think so! Thomas wanted to put 'em on the waiter and carry 'em up himself, but I wouldn't let him. Just look here!"

There were six, at least, for each of the little girls, three for Miss Harson and quite a budget for Malcolm. These had all come from the post-office, but the watch and the rings had not come in that way. Every one in the house had sent a valentine to each of the children, and very pretty valentines they were. The little ones enjoyed them so much that it was a pleasure to see them, and Malcolm laughed a good deal over the one he received. When Miss Harson opened two highly-decorated envelopes addressed to herself, Clara and Edith exchanged significant glances.

"Two of the very prettiest valentines I have seen," said the young lady, with a smile; "and it is so pleasant to be remembered by one's friends!"

"Aren't valentines sometimes just alike?" asked Edith, thinking it would be a pity to let Miss Harson guess right away where they came from.

"Oh yes, indeed! A great many of one kind are always made," replied her governess; but even if she had not remembered so well the flowers and the verses, she could scarcely mistake Malcolm's sprawling handwriting on the two envelopes, for each little sister had applied to him to direct them and get them safely into the post-office.

Miss Harson also had an affectionate

valentine with a number of verses in it from
Malcolm himself, and she said that she intended to put all three away in her portfolio, for she liked them very much indeed.

"One good thing," said Clara, looking
around at her companions: "no one has
guessed who's sent 'em anything—except
papa's presents.—I forgot about yours,
Edie; it's ever so pretty."

"So's yours," was the reply; and then
they both laughed.

"I think you might have sent *me* one,"
said Malcolm, quite reproachfully and with
a disappointed look.

"Why, we did!" exclaimed his sisters
together; "we each sent you one."

Malcolm laughed mischievously; while
Clara groaned:

"Isn't that too bad! to go and tell! But
I know you yourself sent us each one."

"Of course I did; do you think I'd neglect my sisters?"

All were laughing together now, and no
one seemed to be in any doubt as to where
all the valentines had come from. There

was a great deal of enjoyment through the house over them, and John, the gardener, was especially pleased with one addressed to him, in which the verses began with " Fair creature." Clara explained that the verses were not written for him, as they had come already printed, but there were so many colored flowers on the sheet that they thought it would just suit him. The worthy man declared that it suited him elegantly, and that he did not at all mind being called a " fair creature."

All were ready to contribute to the en-joyment of the little invalids, and Kitty made a wonderful cake—which was really only a very nice rusk, as anything richer was not desirable for them—and over it she put a thin icing, with two queer little figures on top, of the same material. Clara and Edith said they looked like doughnut babies, but Kitty said they were meant for Cupids, "there seemed to be so many of 'em flyin' round that day."

" I am sure these couldn't fly," observed Edith, quite seriously, as she bit into one of the dumpy little figures ; and papa and

Miss Harson laughed heartily, while they quite agreed with her.

"We've had such a pleasant day!" said the hospital patients when it was nearly bedtime, "and we are wondering, Miss Harson, what you are going to tell us about this evening."

"Something, dear children, that you have never heard of before, and I have known about it only a very little while myself. It is some work for you to do when the right time comes."

The wide-open eyes did not look at all sleepy, and their little owners wondered what the work could possibly be.

"You have seen," continued their governess, "how much pleasure can be given by unexpected letters—even such as these valentines, which are often very silly; but there are other letters, with blessed words of comfort in them, which can be sent to the poor and the wicked and the sick and the lonely, and do them a good. These are sent by the Christmas-Letter Mission. They were all written by a good lady in

England, who had quantities of them printed
and sent all over the land. At first these
letters were only for the sick people in hospitals, for whom Miss Elliott felt very sorry.
On Christmas eve a letter was placed,
the last thing at night, on the pillow of
each patient, so that it might be seen the
first thing in the morning. Think! if you
were sick and poor and away among
strangers in a hospital—and, worst of all,
knew little or nothing of the blessed Saviour—would it not comfort you to get a
letter, even though written by an unknown
friend, telling you of that heavenly home
where pain and sickness never enter?"

"Yes, indeed, Miss Harson," replied
Clara, earnestly. "But are the letters all
for grown people?"

"Certainly not, dear, as there are always
children in hospitals, as well as in other
places. There are Christmas letters for
sick children and for well ones; for, you
see, after a time people in other institu-
tions besides hospitals heard of these letters and how comforting they were, and
asked why they too could not have them.

Then more letters were written and printed—letters for children in schools and orphan asylums, letters for old people, letters
for all sorts of people.   These letters were
a comfort wherever they went, and sometimes even wicked people in the prisons
would receive them and read them carefully, and think over the kind words until
their hearts were touched and they resolved
to forsake their evil courses.   It was like
preaching a sermon to them all for themselves.   By and by the Christmas letters
came to this country, and a friend has lately written to me, and sent me one to show
what they are like.   Christmas is over, she
says, for this year, but it will be here again
before we know it, and she wishes me to
tell her if I am willing to help her for next
year.   The printed letters, with different-
colored envelopes and a pretty little Christmas card to go in each one, are sold in pack-
ages.   This one is a letter for a sick child in
a hospital.   See how pretty it is."

The children were very much pleased
with the large pink envelope and the
colored card inside, and at the top of the

letter there was a picture of the Good
Shepherd very much like that on the wall,
with a little lamb in his arms and the sheep
around him. The direction on the envelope was printed to look like writing, and
it said, "A Christmas Letter For You."

"Would you like me to read you the
letter, or a part of it?" asked Miss Harson.

"Yes, please," replied both voices; "we
should like to hear it all."

"We will see," replied their governess.
"It is rather long, but I will begin at the
beginning. I know you will think it a very
sweet letter for a poor sick child to receive.
It is dated 'Christmas Eve,' and it says affectionately:

"'DEAR CHILD: Last night, when you
were folded into bed and a kind voice
said, "Go to sleep," you thought to yourself, "To-morrow will be Christmas day!"
And now Christmas day has come, and
here is a letter on your pillow to say, "A
happy Christmas to you!" And here inside the letter is a pretty card saying the
same thing.

"'Who brought you the letter? Was it
the postman? I do not think so. Once
some children who found letters like this
on their pillows said, "The fairies brought
them," but I do not think that any fairy
has been by your bed in the night.

"'Shall I tell you the secret quite in a
whisper? Well, a kind friend has been
thinking about you, and has been saying,
"This little one is sick and weak and away
from father and mother, and so I will send
a letter which shall bring a message the
first thing in the morning," and the message is, "A happy Christmas to you, dear
child!"

"'It is a strange Christmas to you, is it
not? Perhaps last year you were playing
with your brothers and sisters on Christmas
day, but now you are in a little bed in a
large room, and are, it may be, feeling very
sick and tired; and the little head aches,
and you say, "I don't want to play; I would
rather lie still." It may be that you think
you cannot have a happy Christmas like
other children who are running about, but
this letter is sent to tell you that One who

loves you dearly, One who loves you better than even mother loves you, is thinking about you and wants to make you happy, and is close by you, to spend your Christmas, and all other days, with you.

"'Can you guess who it is that I mean? It is Jesus—the same Jesus who was a little child here long, long ago, and who comes down still (though we cannot see him) to comfort every child who wants his love and who says, "Come, Lord Jesus, and save me, and be my friend!"

"'Do you know why Jesus came down to this sad world, in which there is so much pain and sorrow? This was the reason: There was sin in the world. Everybody had gone astray from God. Children, instead of being holy and loving and pleasing their tender Father in heaven, had sinful hearts and bad thoughts, and God had said that no sinful thing should be allowed to go inside the gates of the happy city where he wants you and me and all who love him to live with him for ever. So his own Son Jesus Christ, who knew how happy and glorious was the home

with the Father, came down to this world
—for God loved the world so much that
he did not spare his own dear Son—and
began his life as a baby in a manger at
Bethlehem, and lived on earth thirty-three
years, and then died on the cross to save
sinners. When he died on the cross, it
was to take the punishment of our sins.
His Father said that he would not let the
punishment come upon Jesus and upon
sinners too; it was enough that his own
dear Son should bear all the anger against
sin in our stead. And because he died for
our sins every one who asks to be forgiven
for Jesus Christ's sake, and who wants to
be a child of God, goes quite free and
knows that the loving Father in heaven
has forgiven all that was wrong and
sinful.

"'Jesus our Lord, when he died on the
cross, cried, "It is finished!" which meant
that he had borne all the punishment that
we deserved. And then, after he had been
buried, he rose again out of the grave and
went up into heaven, and said he would be
getting all things ready in "the beautiful

home over there" for every one who comes
to him, for every child who asks to be forgiven. Those children come to him who
from the heart say, " Heavenly Father, I am
a poor sinful child, but thy dear Son died
on the cross instead of me, and I ask that
his death may be counted as the punishment for my sins, and that I may have a
home with thee in heaven for his sake.
And while I am down here teach me to
show how much I thank thee for sending
Jesus to be my Saviour by being obedient
and loving and like him. Hear me for
Jesus Christ's sake. Amen."

"'Now, it was to tell the good news of
Jesus Christ having been born to be a Saviour for sinners that the angels came to
the shepherds who kept their flocks out
of doors on the green hills. And this is
the good news which makes Christmas so
happy to all that love Jesus, and who have
laid all their sin on him.

"'Is it not good news for you, dear child?
Is it not grand to think that your Father in
heaven loves you so much, and wants so
much to have you with him, that he did all

11

this to make it easy for you to come to him here, and right for you to have a place by and by with him in heaven? So now, on this Christmas day, you can sing:

> " ' " I am so glad that our Father in heaven
> Tells of his love in the book he has given;
> Wonderful things in the Bible I see,
> But this is the dearest—that Jesus loves me."

You would like to thank him, would you not, for giving his Son to be your Saviour? You can thank him if you put your hands together and say, "I thank thee, loving Father, for giving thy dear Son Jesus Christ to be my Saviour."

" ' Let me tell you of some children who in a hospital over the sea loved this kind Saviour. They had once been poor little outcast children in the streets of Dublin, but kind friends had taken them out of the streets, and had made them happy in a nice home where they were taught to read and write and to know of Him who died for them. They had such nice playtimes, too, for their friends gave them pretty toys— dolls and cups and saucers and wooden houses—and once a year they went into the country and had dinner and tea away amongst the trees and the flowers.

"'Well, some of these little ones were taken ill with measles, and at last there were thirteen of them all sent to the hospital. One of the kind ladies who went to see them said, "I asked the porter if he could tell me where the 'home' children were. 'I don't know,' he replied. Then, after thinking a minute, he said, 'Perhaps you mean the singing children?'—'Oh yes,' I replied. Then he led me across a yard and rang a bell. Soon the nurse appeared. 'This lady wants to see the "home" children.' Like the porter, she too looked rather puzzled. 'You mean the singing children,' she said, and quickly brought me up stairs into a ward where there were five of the little boys. Only one seemed ill; the others were as bright as possible, ready to sing or repeat texts, or anything else. In another ward were eight little girls, all getting well. Nurse was almost sorry for this. 'I don't know what we shall ever do without them,' she said; and a poor woman in a bed in the corner joined her. 'I am glad they don't disturb you,' I said.—'Oh no ; it is such a pleasure to listen to them ! They keep on singing and saying those lovely verses. And such *clean* children ! Will you tell me, ma'am, how they are kept so clean and so happy ?'—'I think it must be because they are so sure that Jesus loves them, poor wee things ! and because they are so well cared for. He says, " My servants shall sing for joy of heart." ' "

" ' Now, dear child, would you like to be one of the " singing children "? If you are too weak and your head aches too much to sing out loud, you are one of the singing children if in your heart there are thanks to the Lord Jesus for all his love to you in coming to be your Saviour, the " Good Shepherd " of the sheep. And if you are trying to please him by being obedient and bearing your pain bravely, and by trying to do patiently all that your doctor and your nurse tell you to do, he knows that you are trying to show forth your thanks not only with your lips, but with your life ; and this makes the Lord Jesus glad about you.

"'Here is one of the hymns which the singing children learnt to sing:

" ' " There came a little Child to earth
        Long ago,
And the angels of God proclaimed his birth,
        High and low.
Out on the night, so calm and still,
        Their song was heard,
For they knew that the Child on Bethlehem's hill
        Was Christ the Lord.

     *   *   *   *   *   *

" ' " Far away, in a goodly land
        Fair and bright,
Children with crowns of glory stand
        Robed in white—
In white more pure than the spotless snow;
        And their tongues unite
In the psalms which the angels sang long ago
        On Christmas night.

" ' " They sing how the Lord of this world so fair
        A child was born,
And that they might a crown of glory wear
        Wore a crown of thorn,
And in mortal weakness, in want and pain,
        Came forth to die
That the children of earth might for ever reign
        With him on high.

" ' " He has put on his kingly apparel now,
        In that goodly land,
And he leads to where fountains of water flow
        That chosen band;

And for evermore, in their garments fair
    And undefiled,
These ransomed children His praises declare
    Who was once a child."

"'I must not write any more now, but I should like to tell you the story of little Alice, who was one of the singing children, and who went to be with Jesus in the "goodly land." The lady at the home wrote :

"'"Just twelve months ago now a very poor woman came leading by the hand a pale, delicate-looking child of seven years old. She was her only child, and she said that they were starving together. We had no room in the home for little Alice, and we advised the mother to send her to the Ragged School daily, to try and get work for a few months, and when winter came we would try and make room for the little one, while her mother could then go to service and help to support her. Months passed away, and we saw no more of little Alice, except that we saw her pale face among the hundred other poor children in the Luke Street infant school. One day just about Christ-

mas a kind-hearted doctor told us that
there was in the hospital a little girl in
rapid consumption, the result of starva-
tion and misery; the child said she belonged to the Luke Street school. I went
to visit her. There were four beds in the
ward—women in three of them. In the
fourth a child lay sleeping, and I knew
little Alice. As I gazed at the wasted
form and the little white face my heart
was filled with sorrow, for I thought of
the day she had been brought to our
door when we could not take her in.
As I stood there, very sad, the child
awoke. She looked at me, then, with a
bright smile, sat up. I spoke to her, but
she put her hand to her ear. She could
scarcely catch a word of what I said, but,
knowing what I meant, she said brightly,
'I'm very ill, but.I'm not afraid; I'm

" Safe in the arms of Jesus,
Safe on his gentle breast." '

She knew a great many texts of Scripture;
and when I raised my voice so that she
could hear, she would answer in the loved

words. She believed in the Father's love
when 'he gave his only begotten Son;'
she trusted in Jesus' kindness: 'Him that
cometh to me, I will in no wise cast out;'
she knew her perfect safety—the Lord her
Shepherd. Dear little Alice! we had no
room for her in our home, but Jesus put
his Holy Spirit into her heart, and soon
he called her to the mansion he had prepared for her.

> ' In the bright and golden region,
>   With its pearly gates so fair,
> She is singing with the angels:
>   There is room for Alice there.' "

"'And there is room for *you* there, dear
child. Oh, come to the Saviour! Make
no delay. May he make your Christmas
day happy, dear child, with his love!

"'I am your affectionate friend,

"'_____.'"

"Dear little Alice!" murmured Edith,
softly, when Miss Harson had finished
reading.

"And what a lovely long letter to get!"

said Clara. "I should think the sick children would be delighted with such letters."

"They do seem to like them very much,"
replied her governess, "and well children
are equally pleased. In an orphan asylum
where this friend who wrote to me sent letters last Christmas the children themselves
asked the matron to write and thank the
kind lady for remembering them in that
way. Some of the accounts of the grown
people are very touching; one poor woman
said that she had not received a letter before
for thirty years."

"Wasn't that dreadful?" said the children. "We shouldn't like not to get a
letter for thirty years. But can't we send
some, Miss Harson, to people who don't
get any?"

"Yes, dears, you can," was the reply.
"You shall send some to St. John's Hospital next Christmas if you like; I know
they will be glad of them there."

"Why, it's just like valentines," said
Edie, "only these are Christmas letters.
But people don't know who send 'em."

"It's better than valentines," corrected

Clara, "and I wish that Christmas would hurry around again, for I want so much to send some that I don't feel as if I could wait."

CHAPTER XI.

"SNOW! snow! snow!" exclaimed glee-ful voices the next morning, and snow, snow, snow, it was. Great flakes like feathers and small ones like diamonds came flying down in a wild, whirling sort of way, looking, as Clara said, as though they enjoyed it. Old Winter was evidently determined to keep young Spring back as long as he could, and every one exclaimed, "What a contrast the weather is to that of yesterday!" But the hospital people were wonderfully cheerful over it, and began to talk about going down stairs and getting out of the ward altogether. Dr. Gates, however, who still came to see them, did not approve of this; he said that his little patients must make haste slowly, which seemed to them a very curious way of making haste.

"I'd really like to have the measles my-self," he added, comically, "and rest a while in this pleasant hospital, where people could not drag me out in all sorts of weather just because they happened to be sick. Why, I don't have any time to be sick ; I never dare try anything more than a headache, be-cause I would not be allowed to finish it out."

The doctor looked quite sorrowful over it, and Edie said that he was a funny man, to want to be sick.

"That isn't the part that I want, so much as the comfort of being let alone," replied he, laughing, "and having the chance to enjoy such a pleasant room. But, after all, if I *were* sick, I would not have any Miss Harson, you see, to make a lovely hospital like this for me."

"Wouldn't Mrs. Gates?" asked Clara, as the little girls were beginning to feel quite sorry for the doctor.

"No, I do not believe she would ever think of it; and if she did, she could not find any of my dolls to make it look like a ward. I did not keep any."

The children were now laughing merrily, although Dr. Gates tried to look sober over his misfortunes, and Miss Harson laughed too when he spoke of his dolls.

"Now," continued the doctor, "I know exactly what you two little plotters are thinking of in this sudden haste to get down stairs as soon as the snow comes: you are thinking of a sleighride."

Clara and Edith exchanged glances, and then looked at the doctor in the most beseeching way.

"Now, listen," said he: "if you are very good indeed, you may have a sleighride next July—if there is enough snow. Well," as the faces clouded over so suddenly that there seemed to be. danger of a shower, "perhaps I *could* say a little sooner. How would to-morrow do?"

Dr. Gates was down stairs almost as soon as he had finished the sentence, leaving his patients in a state of delightful excitement. They went around the ward and told all the dolls that they were going and were sorry they could not take them too.

"You may take one doll and a kitten apiece," said Miss Harson, "if you think you can keep them comfortable and not drop them out of the sleigh."

Of course the little girls thought so, but there was some trouble in choosing the dolls. As they had only one kitten apiece, that question was easily enough decided; but it was no trifle to hurt the feelings of twelve dolls because only two could be taken. The prime favorites, Isabel and Rosaletta, were too big, and finally a wild-looking creature who was very ill with scarlet-fever, and a small worsted child afflicted with the croup, were selected because "the fresh air would do them good." Miss Harson said laughingly that the air was generally considered bad for such complaints, but that she did not think it would do any serious harm in this case.

The next morning dawned bright and beautiful, and at an early hour Malcolm was shouting under one of the windows, "All right, chicks! Weather perfectly splendid!" Then there were two or three "Hurrahs!" and the little girls were now quite roused and feeling as if something very delightful were going to happen. But there was plenty of time, for Dr. Gates said that they must take their ride in the warmest part of the day, and this is always from twelve to three. After an early dinner there was a great jingling of sleighbells outside, and the voices of Malcolm and Thomas, who evidently disagreed about something. The young gentleman wanted to drive, and Thomas objected.

Presently the would-be coachman came dashing into the ward to see how nearly his sisters were ready:

"It takes a good while to pack 'em up, doesn't it, Miss Harson? What bundles they look like! Shouldn't think they could breathe. I'm glad I ain't a girl and that I didn't have measles."

Each little sister had on two or three outer garments and a warm hood, with a white Shetland veil pinned over her face; also thick leggins and fur capes and mittens. "Rose" and "Daisy," the kittens, wore suits of fur and an extra wrap (of ribbon) round their necks. The

two dolls appeared to be going in their
night-dresses, but they were not at all
disturbed by it.

It was a lovely winter's day, cold, but not
with a sting in it. The banks of snow by
the roadside seemed to have a coating of
ice that made them flash and sparkle in
the sunshine as though they were studded
with diamonds. Thomas had carefully carried each little mummy down stairs and put
her in a sitting posture in the comfortable
sleigh, with a kitten in one arm and a doll
in the other, looking too happy to speak.
Miss Harson was happy, too, that her little charges were able to get the fresh air,
and Malcolm, although he *would* tease
them now and then, was quite delighted
to have his sisters out again. He thought
they were all right now, but they were still
weak, and their enjoyment of the ride did
not prevent their getting tired in a short
time.

As soon as everything was settled away
dashed the sleigh and its occupants, flying
past the posts and fences so rapidly that
the horses almost seemed to have wings

A Merry Sleighride. Page 176.

to their feet. The dogs came out and
barked at them as they passed farmhouses
and country-seats, and the children laughed
to see how angry they were that they could
not catch the horses.

A muffled voice came from under Clara's
veil, saying,

"I'm glad we've got so many sleighbells;
it seems like riding to music.—Can we
drive past Mrs. Purse's, Miss Harson?"

"Certainly, dear, if you wish it.—We
will take the road by Poverty Row,
Thomas.—But do not talk in this cold
air except when it is necessary."

Clara obediently sank back in her corner and watched the dark woods on each
side of the road; she would not like, she
thought, to be walking there *now*, much as
she loved to see the graceful trees in summer.

"Do wolves come out here in winter?"
she asked; but Miss Harson put her finger
to her lip (as well as a mitten would let her)
and shook her head.

The next moment there was a loud
scream from poor Edie, who had turned

her head and reached over to watch something that was moving in the woods as Clara spoke, and before she knew it she had tumbled out in the snow. But the snow was soft, and she did not get hurt, only pretty well frightened, and her governess now held her so tightly that she could not very easily fall out again. Thomas had picked her up in a flash, and then the worsted doll, but Daisy was all right. Like the sensible little kitten that she was, she had dug her claws into some of the soft woolen things around her little mistress and hung on for dear life, for she seemed to know that to land on that cold snow would be anything but comfortable. Edith scarcely felt it, either, because she was so well wrapped up, but she seemed disposed, after her tumble, to cling as tightly to Miss Harson as Daisy clung to her.

Malcolm had taken the reins when Thomas got out of the sleigh, and he now begged so hard just to drive past Poverty Row that his governess consented.

"Do not forget what precious freight you

have here," she said, laughingly; "and if any of the rest of us tumble out, we must go directly home."

"*I* sha'n't tumble out," replied Malcolm, with an answering laugh, "but I don't see how I can keep the rest of you from doing it."

The sentence was scarcely finished when Malcolm lost his balance, and was saved from a roll in the snow, and perhaps from a kick from the horses' feet, only by clinging to the dashboard. Thomas seized the reins just in time, and helped the young gentleman to his seat.

"What was the matter?" asked Miss Harson, very quietly.

"I thought I saw a rabbit skimming along over there close by the edge of the woods," replied Malcolm, looking rather confused, "and so—"

"You forgot your duty," interposed his governess, "and risked the danger of upsetting the sleigh. This may help you to understand why we never feel quite safe when you have the reins.—And please remember, Thomas, that Mr. Malcolm is to do no more driving until he has express permission from his father."

" I will, ma'am," answered Thomas, feeling quite relieved ; he was very fond of "the young gentleman," but he did not like to trust his driving.

Malcolm felt that his sentence was only right, and, instead of sulking over the punishment, as some boys would have done, he told Miss Harson that he was sorry, and was as bright and pleasant-tempered as possible. People could not help loving the lad in spite of his troublesome faults, and his little sisters thought that very few brothers were as nice as this one of theirs.

When Poverty Row was reached, every one of its population that could do so was looking out from the windows, and all the Purses rushed out on the steps and waved things at the sleighriders. Janey, who was quite well now, waved a red plaid shawl, and Mrs. Purse, who did not seem to know exactly what she was doing, waved the baby. The youngest girl had a large check apron in her hand, and the small boy blew vigorously on a tin trumpet. The poor people

were so earnest and hearty in their gladness to see the little invalids out again that
they must show it in some way; and their
way meant just as much as did that of people who could better express their feelings.
Miss Harson could not help laughing, but
she stopped the sleigh for a moment and
spoke very kindly to them all, · while the
two bundles beside her were giggling with
delight, for they were too tired to do anything more. They even heard the order,
"Now a short turn to the left, and then
home again, Thomas," without feeling sorry,
though the sleighride had been such a treat
to them.

Clara and Edith were very glad to get
back into their little blue wrappers again
and lie down in the pleasant ward; their
kind governess knew that it would be so,
and she had everything ready to make
them comfortable. She knew, too, that
it would be a long time yet before her
little girls could feel as strong and well
as they did before they were taken ill.
Fast asleep were both before long, and so
were the kittens. Miss Harson and Mal-

colm went out for a walk, and the clock ticked away in the hospital with all its might, as though it was endeavoring not to feel lonely.

CHAPTER XII.

TRYING TO WORK.

THE two little patients found that they could not go down stairs and run about as usual, because they had been out in the air; indeed, they were so tired the day after that pleasant sleighride that they did not even sit up much of the time in the ward. Dr. Gates came in to see, as he said, if they were still alive, and he added that they were doing very well indeed, and that this was what he meant by making haste slowly.

"Next time," said he, "you will not feel quite so tired, for we will not try it again too soon, though I mean that you shall have another and a longer sleighride; and if we go on carefully, you will be well again almost before you know it. Let me see: the kittens haven't taken the measles, have

183

they?" for they too were languid and did not care to move.

But this idea amused the children very much. How could Dr. Gates tell whether the kittens had measles or not, under all that fur, and with no pulses to feel and not sense enough to put out their tongues? Leaving very smiling faces behind him, the kind doctor went on his rounds among the other sick people.

In a few days the little sisters seemed stronger and brighter for their ride and were once more on the mend. They were much interested, too, in some pretty patch-work which Miss Harson had arranged for them, but she would let them do only a very little at a time, for fear of their tiring and hurting themselves. They liked to sort out the bright-colored silks and ribbons and to do the simple embroidery-stitches which they had just learned. It seemed all the nicer to do it because Miss Harson had just been telling them of a silk patchwork-quilt that was made at the hospital by the sick children and finished in time to hang it up, on Donation Day, where it could be seen by the numerous visitors. Then it was voted who should have it, and every one who voted paid twenty-five cents, which was put into the fund for the Heart's-Ease Cot. Some small girls and one little boy worked at the quilt and did their very best to make the squares neat and pretty.

" The little boy's pieces were remarkably nice," said the lady who wrote about the quilt in the *Heart's-Ease*, "and this is how it was all done: A kind young-lady friend of the hospital procured a number of pretty silk and velvet pieces and showed the Little Mother and the wee bairns how to baste them in squares. Then she gave them the embroidery-silk, and they all learned how to use that. The Little Mother, you may be sure, worked very hard, and helped the others to learn too. When the quilt was lined and hung up, they could hardly believe they had made it. Every one admired the handsome quilt, and the voting went on briskly. When the sum of thirty-eight dollars was realized, the evening was ended; and who do you think received the greatest number of votes and became the

happy owner of the quilt? Why, the Little Mother, and very dear it will ever be to
her, you may be sure. So there have gone
into the endowment fund thirty-eight dollars, earned through the assistance of one
young lady and the little sick ones themselves. And thus they, too, have taken
their share in the great work of relieving
the sufferings of others, and that work will
go on and on when they are all gone from
the sunny home they now rest in."

The children were then more anxious
than ever to do some good, and as they
were talking about these things their governess glanced at the row of tiny beds on
each side of the larger ones, and said,

"I suppose the other hospital patients,
too, will be getting better soon?"

"They are a great deal better now," was
the reply, "and they are going to get quite
well just as soon as we do."

"That is very obliging of them," continued Miss Harson. "And where are they
going to live when they get out of the
hospital?"

Clara and Edith had not thought of this,

and appeared to have nothing to say for themselves.

"Let me read you some verses," said their governess, "which I think you will like;" and the little girls were only too glad to listen to

"THE DOLL'S MISSION.

"Yes, Fido ate Annabel's head off:
I really suppose she is dead;
And Dora has swallowed her eyeballs,
And Claire has a crack in her head.

"But Eva has gone on a mission—
A regular mission, not fun;
She lives at the hospital yonder,
And wears a gray dress like a nun.

"As soon as I heard of the children—
The poor little sick ones, you know—
With nothing at all to amuse them,
I knew 'twas her duty to go.

"I loved her the best of my dollies:
Her eyes were the loveliest blue;
But doing your duty 'most always
Means something you'd rather not do.

"And when I remember the children—
So tired and lonesome and sad—
If I had a houseful of dollies,
I'd give them the best that I had."

"And now, Edie," said Clara, in quite a business-like way, when they had thanked Miss Harson for the verses, "how many shall we send?"

"All," replied Edith, in a rather choked voice, "except Isabel and Rosaletta; we couldn't let them go on a mission, could we?"

"No," said her governess, "I don't think you could. And, besides, they are such very elegant young ladies that they would be quite unsuitable. It would not be at all selfish for each of you to keep one or two of the others; I only thought that out of your abundance you might contribute to those who have none."

The two bright faces looked very much relieved now, and the girls at once began to select the dollies that were to go to the hospital and those that were to stay. The little sisters, after some whispering over the small beds, declared that they would keep only one doll apiece, besides the two favorites, and that they wished they could do a great deal more than that for the poor sick children.

"The wish to do good is the most important thing," replied Miss Harson, "and with the Christmas-letter mission, and other plans that we are making, I think you will have work enough for two little girls. I have a story here about two sisters who were anxious to help and what they found to do, and I know I need not ask if you would like to hear it."

"No, indeed!" exclaimed Clara; "only please tell us, Miss Harson, if you wrote it."

"Yes," replied her governess, "I believe I did; and it is called

"A WILL AND A WAY.

"'I don't believe we can do anything,' said a disconsolate voice.

"'*I* do,' replied a cheery one; 'we can do lots of things. Don't you remember that story about a boy who heard a sermon on Sunday asking people to give something to build a church, if it was only a single brick, and how, bright and early on Monday morning, he trundled a brick in his wheelbarrow up to the minister's door? And then, you know, though people laugh-

ed a good deal when they heard of it, they
began to feel ashamed, because the boy had
done what he could, while they had done
nothing. So every one went around to
every one else, and talked and consulted
about it, and pretty soon the minister had
a lot of money for the building ; and it was
partly owing, you see, to the boy and his
brick.'

"'Well, Nellie Baker, do you think *we'd*
better go and wheel a brick up to somebody's door ?'

"'No, Susie Baker, I don't; but we might
do something else, if we could only think
of anything. We've got to think of something if we expect ever to get that cot in
the hospital endowed.'

"'What is "endowed"?' asked Susie.

"'Why, you know, it's—it's a bed that
some child can stay in all the time, you see,
because somebody gives the money to pay
for it; and Miss Alice wants all our class to
help pay for the Heart's-Ease Cot. I don't
see why we can't do something as well as
the other girls. We might have a strawberry-shortcake party, if mother is willing.'

"'What good would that do?' said the younger sister.

"'Why, you see,' continued Nellie, brightly, 'every one thinks that mother's strawberry-shortcake is so nice, and perhaps people would pay a good deal of money to come and eat as much as they wanted. Only, Maria's pretty cross, you know, and she's the one that really makes it. I'm going to ask her now.'

"In rushed two rosy, excited little girls to the clean, shaded kitchen and attacked the neat but rather cross-appearing woman who was hulling a great pile of fresh-looking strawberries.

"'Oh, Maria,' began Nellie, in headlong fashion, 'will you not make us twelve very big strawberry-shortcakes?'

"'No, I will not,' replied Maria, promptly, 'and you ought to be ashamed of yourselves to ask me such a thing. You get enough strawberry-shortcake, in all conscience, as it is, to make any reasonable children sick.'

"This was not encouraging, and Maria would listen to no explanations; so away

went the two little sisters, very angry indeed, to complain to their mother of
Maria's crossness.

"'I think you are all cross,' replied Mrs.
Baker when she had heard the story, 'and
that certainly is not the way to begin a
good work. But I will think over this
shortcake plan; and if it seems best to
undertake it, I have no doubt that Maria
can be persuaded to help us. But what do
Nellie and Susie Baker propose doing toward it themselves?'

"'We'll do anything,' said Nellie, eagerly. 'We might pick all the strawberries.'

"'And hull them,' added Susie, who
hated the work.

"Mamma saw that the girls were in
earnest, and, as she believed that the
strawberry-shortcake festival might be
successfully managed, she went to talk
with Maria about it.

"'Bless their little hearts!' exclaimed
Maria, in great admiration. 'So that's what
they wanted the twelve strawberry-shortcakes for, is it? Why didn't they tell me
so?'

" Nellie felt like replying that she would not let them; but when Maria happened to be in a good humor, it was wiser not to risk a change.

" The children worked very hard indeed, for was it not their 'very own plan,' as mamma said? And did it not seem delightful that they could really help to endow another cot at the hospital? Young as they were, they knew that there was very little money left in their home after they were fed and clothed. Mrs. Baker could not wear a sealskin sacque and diamond earrings, like some of the girls' mothers, but she always said laughingly that she did not care for these things, and what she really wanted was more money to give away.

" Maria did make twelve big short cakes, after all, and they were better than ever. The festival was held in the shady garden, and the strawberries were gathered from the Bakers' own beds, which were so large that quarts and quarts could be picked without your missing them. Nellie's back ached and her fingers and

13

Susie's were stained a very pretty color, but not one that is fashionable for fingers. Mrs. Baker, too, was tired, and Maria declared that she was just turning into a great strawberry-shortcake. But all that could came to the festival and praised the strawberry-shortcake, and they laughed as they said that they were 'so glad to eat it for the sake of the hospital.' They wondered, too, what people would think of next to endow one of those cots that they were for ever hearing about.

"How Nellie and Susie danced with glee when their mother counted up the money and told them how much it was—quite a pile of dollars—and said that she never would have thought of such a plan herself! The best of it all was that it set ever so many more people thinking and made them feel that they too would be willing to get tired to help pay for one of those pretty blue beds in the Children's Ward."

"That's just as nice as it can be, Miss

Harson," exclaimed the children, enthusiastically. "Can't we have a strawberry-
shortcake festival next summer and give
the money to the Heart's-Ease Cot?"

The governess was expecting this, and
answered kindly:

"You can do something else in place of
a festival—papa would not quite approve
of that, I think—and while you are in the
home hospital we can make our plans and
be all ready to go to work as soon as you
are strong enough."

"Any way," said Edie, "the dolls can go,
and that will be something."

"Yes," replied Miss Harson, "it will
make a very good beginning;" and, with
her youngest charge in her arms and
Clara nestled close beside her, she sat
there in the pleasant firelight until Jane
came up with the tea-tray.

CHAPTER XIII.

MAKING THE BEST OF IT.

THE next morning Mr. Kyle said that he was coming home from town early on purpose to take his little girls out sleigh-riding, and that they must be all ready to jump in when the sleigh returned from the station with him.

"Whoever tumbles out," he added, "will have to be left in the snow."

The children laughed unconcernedly at this, for, in the first place, no one meant to tumble out; and if any one did, there was not much danger of being left behind. But papa, they declared, was getting so nice and funny that they had ever such good times with him.

Two more bundles, as Malcolm said, were packed up carefully, but with a little help the bundles walked down stairs this time

instead of being carried, and papa lifted
them into the sleigh and tucked them up
with the buffalo-robes. Miss Harson did
not go, because she was not needed now,
and she preferred taking a walk to the village; but Malcolm sprang up beside Thomas in high glee, for he was always ready for
a sleighride.

The snow was as beautiful as ever and
looked as though it had come to stay for
some time, and the little girls felt so much
better than they did on the first ride that
they enjoyed every moment of it. They
could scarcely believe it when Mr. Kyle
said they had gone six miles and he was
afraid to keep them out any longer at
once; but when he added that this snow
would last and they should have more
sleighrides over it yet, they looked bright
and happy again and went home without
a murmur.

"I shouldn't wonder, Edie," said Clara,
the last thing before they went to sleep
that night, "if we could go as much as ten
miles the next time—perhaps to-morrow.
Will it not be lovely?"

Edith was almost too sleepy to answer, but this brilliant idea roused her a little, and she managed to murmur, "Yes."

Next morning a dreary plash was the first sound that every one heard—a steady pouring down of rain upon the beautiful snow, and such a dark, dismal rain that Kitty had to keep the gas in the kitchen lighted long past the hour when generally it was extinguished.

"How disappointed those two mites up stairs will be!" thought the good creature as she got them an extra-tempting breakfast. "Just as they were getting out again, too, and counting on such good times with the snow! I declare, it makes me 'most mad to see the rain."

Unfortunately, it made the "mites" quite mad; they pushed away their breakfast and cried, and Jane declared that they were real naughty. Miss Harson knew that she had two nervous little invalids to deal with, and she was very kind and gentle, but she looked quite pained as she went around trying to make them comfortable and happy. After watching

her for a little while Clara suddenly
asked,

"Is it wicked, Miss Harson, to be sorry
that it rains?"

"No, dear," was the reply; "we cannot
help being sorry when we are disappointed.
But if, because we are disappointed in one
thing, we refuse to enjoy any of the bless-
ings left to us and spend our time in crying
and complaining, is not that like being un-
grateful to God?"

"I never thought of it before," said the
little girl, "but I'm afraid that it is; we'll
try not to be naughty any more. You do
not know, though, Miss Harson, how Edie
and I had counted on another sleighride to-
day, and now I don't believe we'll get one
this whole winter."

"That was just your complaint before
you had any ride," answered her governess, "and yet, in spite of it, you have had
two. Spring will not be here for some time
yet, and we have at least seven more snow-
storms in prospect, if what the paper said
about it is true. But even if there were
to be no more snow, we must remember

that our heavenly Father orders all these things as his divine love and wisdom see to be best, and there are others to be considered besides the people who wish to go sleighriding."

On either side a little hand was slipped into one of Miss Harson's, and, kissing both rosy mouths, which were bravely trying to smile, the young lady said brightly,

"Come, chickabiddies; we'll just see how pleasant a day we can make of it in the house; and of course there's a story, but that doesn't come just yet."

Then, saying something in a whisper to Jane, the young lady wrapped a shawl over the head and shoulders of each little girl and took both of them into the hall for a walk.

"Why, it seems just as if we were going out somewhere," said Clara.

"Suppose that you had to go out in this storm?" replied her governess. "Suppose that you had no papa to take care of you and give you this comfortable home, and that you were forced to go out in all sorts of weather to work or to beg your daily bread? There *are* children who have to do this. But now come; we will walk up and down twelve times in a row, and see if we don't feel better for it."

Of course the girls did—ever so much better; for they just needed a little gentle exercise and change of air, and Miss Harson was so "funny" that they were soon laughing merrily in spite of the rain. This was just what their governess wanted; and when she thought they had walked enough, she said,

"Suppose we go now and see what Jane has prepared for our breakfast?"

The children really believed they were hungry; and when they found that Kitty had sent them up a plate of her nicest batter-cakes, steaming hot, with plenty of sugar and cinnamon to eat upon them, they sat down at the little table with a great deal of satisfaction. Miss Harson did not think they were likely to starve that day.

"Well, pussies," said papa as, muffled in his overcoat, he looked in for a moment, "you have much the best of it to-day; I shall scarcely enjoy my trip to town and back."

"But think of the beautiful snow, papa, all melting away!"

"Think of the beautiful snow that's coming," was the laughing reply, "when you will be well enough to enjoy it."

Malcolm was happy with his tools, being engaged in making something for each of his sisters, and he scarcely showed himself in the hospital until story-telling time. He was generally on hand for that.

After breakfast was cleared away and the room put in nice order, Miss Harson brought out the three large boxes which held the silk patchwork, and the two little girls were busy with that for an hour or two. Then a smaller box was produced, and in this were bunches of beautiful beads which Clara and Edith had never seen before. Their governess had sent to the city for them, so as to have something ready against just such a day as this, and the little invalids were half wild with delight over them. They strung them in all sorts of ways, made bracelets for them-

selves and Miss Harson and ornamented
the entire row of dolls with necklaces, because, as Edie said, their necks were the only
part that showed. While they were doing
this their governess read to them from
A Child's History of England, for they
were able now in this way to keep up a
little with their studies, but care was taken
not to tire the still weak little heads.

"We have had enough history for to-
day," said Miss Harson, after reading a
few pages; "let us go and look out of all
the windows on this floor, and see how the
rain looks from each one of them."

Again the little girls were muffled up,
very much to their amusement, for it
seemed so funny when they were not
even going down stairs; but it would have
been a serious thing for them to take cold
when they were just getting over a severe
attack of measles, and their wise young
governess would not allow them to be
exposed in any way.

Each window seemed to have a different
view, but there were drenched evergreens
and the rain washing away the snow in

little streams from the lawn, "great rivers," as the girls called the puddles in the road, soaked roofs and fences, and now and then some bedraggled hen who seemed to have gotten lost and did not know what to do with herself. At every window the rain was saying fiercely, "Let me in! Let me in!" At least, this is what Edie thought, and it did dash wildly against the panes.

After this walk the hospital looked more pleasant than ever. Clara made a discovery which Miss Harson had made before breakfast, but of which she did not tell the children because she wished them to have the pleasure of finding it out for themselves. Two of the hyacinths were in bloom. A lovely pink cluster of flowers, and an equally lovely white one, had raised their fragrant heads far above the green shoots and the warm moss that sheltered them, and the beautiful waxen bells were full of sweetness. Clara and Edith had often seen hyacinths before—for John had a choice collection every spring—but these were their very own, their hospital flowers,

which bloomed on purpose for them and
had come out to cheer them on this stormy
day. So they made much of the graceful
blossoms; and when they had admired and
petted them to their hearts' content, Miss
Harson emptied the box of letters on the
table, and they sat down to the word-game.
There was a great deal of laughing over
the funny spelling that went on as the
little girls tried hard to make words with
such letters as *X's* and *Y's*, and it seemed
quite cruel for their governess take them
to pieces. But little Edith finally won the
game, with Miss Harson's help, and then,
to their great surprise, Jane came and.
asked if she might have the table for dinner. It had been such a short morning, in
spite of the rain; but had they sat and
worried about the weather, as they began
the day, the hours would have seemed very
long and dreary. After dinner there were
a little more patchwork and reading, and
then it was time for their nap. This lasted
two hours; and when they awoke, it was
getting toward sunset.

"Story-time?" asked Malcolm, in the

doorway. Miss Harson said "Yes," and the young gentleman very promptly walked in.

"You ought to have been here, Malcolm," said Edie as he sat down beside her; "it's been *so* pleasant all day!"

"Delightful!" added Clara. "Miss Harson's been just as sweet as she could be."

"I think she's always sweet," was the reply, "but thank you for wanting me. *I* had a nice time, too, in the tool-room."

"I wonder if I should like being a boy?" said Clara, as though she felt obliged to make up her mind about it. She sometimes thought boys had a great many pleasures out of which girls were kept.

"It doesn't particularly matter, dear," replied her governess, with a smile, "as you will never be called upon to try; and now, if you are all quite ready, I will read you a story which I have called

"A RAINY DAY.

"Grandma Colton was scolding in her funny way. She would like to know, she said, what people meant by coming into the country and acting as if the weather were taking a liberty when it rained. Did they not have rain in the city too? And how could they expect to get food if there should be no rain to make things grow?

"'But the very first day, grandma!' pleaded Bob as an excuse for his complaining. 'We came only last night, you know, and we had planned such grand good times out of doors to-day.'

"'As you will stay at least two months,' replied Grandpa Colton—' for we shall not let you off any sooner—you will have sixty-one days for the grand good times; and you can certainly afford to let it rain a little, when rain is so much needed.'

"'But some of those sixty-one days will be Sundays,' said Uncle George, who liked to tease a little now and then, 'and on some of them Rob and Bertie will be doubled up with cholera morbus—green apples and mother's huckleberry-cake combined; and on some of them it will probably rain worse than it does now. They'll lose about fifteen days altogether.'

"The boys howled at this prospect, and

then rushed upon Uncle George for a grand pounding-match.

"'Now, that's something sensible,' observed grandma, 'if you do make a dreadful racket; anything but moping round and complaining of the weather. If people can't do one thing, they can generally do another; and, at any rate, we must remember that God sends rain or sunshine as it best pleases him, and he knows when it ought to come, too.'

"Just then Aunt Lily, who looked as sweet as her name, came tripping into the room and called out laughingly,

"'Boys! boys! Listen a minute, will you? Poor mamma has a terrible headache from the long journey, and she wishes to know if the band of wild Indians who have invaded the kitchen will not retire to the barn, where they can shout to their hearts' content without disturbing her.'

"'Come on, Uncle George!' said the boys, breathlessly; 'we'll finish you up there.'

"Away they all went, but Uncle George soon 'finished up' his assailants, rolling them over and over in the hay until they were glad just to lie still and laugh.

"There was plenty of work to do on the farm even on rainy days, and Rob and Bertie watched their uncle with great interest as he went around putting things in order.

"'A rainy day now and then,' said he, 'is a perfect blessing, unless there's hay to get in, for things are always getting broken, and in fine weather there seems to be no time to mend them. Remember that, boys, if you ever have a farm of your own.'

"This set the boys to thinking a little. There were people in the world, then, who really enjoyed the rain? and of course their own pleasure could not be considered all the time; so they made up their minds to enjoy it too. They helped Uncle George, and boasted that they got plenty of fun out of him besides.

"It was really a short morning, after all, and mamma had had a comfortable nap, and her headache was better; and grandma had chicken pot-pie for dinner, and

14

cherry-dumplings.   After their work in
the barn Rob and Bertie had such ap-
petites that every one began to fear that
the 'doublings up' which Uncle George had
prophesied could not be far off.   But boys
are very apt to disappoint people on this
score, and Rob and Bertie still continued
in good health.   Mamma said they were
behaving remarkably well, as they were
not at all boisterous; and they certainly
seemed more quiet than usual.

"When Aunt Lily came to sit down with
her basket of bright wools, of which she
was making an afghan, she found her neph-
ews looking over the pictures in a scrap-
book and arguing about one that repre-
sented some Japanese people out in the
rain.

"'I like that picture,' said Rob, 'because
it seems as if it was to-day, the rain is coming down so; but I don't see what that girl
with the long hair hanging down from under her hat has got a kind of a fur skirt on
for.'

"'And I don't see,' said Bertie, 'why that
tall boy wears his trousers so long, and

what he's skating for when it's raining.
Aren't they funny?'

"'Maybe it doesn't rain the same way in
Japan that it does here,' began Rob; but,
seeing that Aunt Lily was laughing over
her work, he stopped to ask what amused
her.

"'You, dears,' replied their frank young
auntie; and then she put aside her work
and gave them each a kiss as she bent
down to examine the picture. 'Oh, I can
tell you all about that,' she continued,
brightly; 'Mr. Loo Kee, the young
Chinese gentleman who belongs to our
Bible class, has explained a great many
such pictures to me.—And first, Rob, I
must tell you that your girl with long hair
and a fur skirt is a man in a waterproof
coat.'

"'Why, it doesn't look a bit like mamma's waterproof,' exclaimed the boys, in
great surprise.

"'No, it is not made of rubber-cloth,
like hers, but of straw or thin wisps of
bamboo, which is a very useful tree to the
Chinese and the Japanese. When people

are dressed in these queer garments, they look as if they were covered with straw; and here, in this little book, is a traveler's description of a Japanese dress for a rainy day. He says: "A peasant was passing who wore a rain-coat. The straw wisps had been ingeniously arranged into a garment that fell over his shoulders and hung down about his person. A bamboo hat was on his head, and he carried a bamboo pole over his shoulder. Coarse, thick socks were on his feet, and bound to these were rough, heavy clogs of wood." You see the clogs in the picture, on the lady's feet, and they look like little benches.'

"'Then my girl is a man,' said Rob, 'and Bertie's tall boy is a lady! I have heard people say that things are upside down in China and Japan, and I should think they were. We don't have anything so funny as waterproofs made of straw, and I should think that the people who wear them would get soaking wet.'

"'On the contrary,' replied Aunt Lily, 'they are kept nice and dry. You see, too, that they thatch themselves with straw,

as if they were houses, only their roofs will
go on and off. The poor lady in the picture has the worst of it, for she wears neither rain-coat nor hat and has only that
queer-looking flat umbrella with which to
protect herself, while the little benches
under her feet must prevent her from
getting along very fast.'

"'I thought she was skating,' said Bertie, 'when she was a boy; and I guess that
Grandma Colton's is the nicest place to be
in when it rains, anyhow.'

"Aunt Lily and Rob both laughed at
Bertie's queer mixing of things, and
grandma herself, who came in just then,
said,

"'So the rainy day has not been quite
a lost day, after all; for, besides making
yourselves useful, you have learned something about rainy weather in another country.'"

"Oh," said Edie, "how very nice that is,
when it's raining here, to hear about some
other children who didn't like to have it
rain, and about their kind auntie and

Japanese waterproofs! And this is the very picture too!"

Clara said it made her feel as if she were in a story herself, and Malcolm wished that it was summer, and that they might go and stay at such a pleasant place as Grandma Colton's.

It had been a day of pleasant things, but there was a surprise at the end that seemed pleasantest of all. About half an hour before dinner Miss Harson and Jane began dressing instead of undressing two little girls. Curls were brushed out and soft, thick dresses put on; bright sashes were tied once more; and Clara and Edith began to think that they were actually going to dine down stairs again with papa and Miss Harson and Malcolm. That was just it, and now they understood why papa had not looked in upon them for a few moments, as he generally did when he came home: he wished to see them first when they were once more dressed to receive him. But they had been up stairs so long now that things down stairs did not look quite natural. And was that

really papa—that gentleman coming forward to meet them with a rose in his but-
tonhole? He looked so tall and grand
that they were almost afraid of him. It
did not take long to get over this feeling
when each little daughter was lifted up for
a loving kiss and a warm welcome, and the
pretty dining-room seemed to look brighter and pleasanter than ever. John had
sent his choicest flowers to decorate the
table, and there was a little bouquet of
mignonette, with a half-blown rose in the
centre, beside each plate. Clara and Edie
knew that they were only visitors yet, and
that to-morrow they might not be able to
come down all day; but they were obediently "making haste slowly," and Dr.
Gates had .said that it would not be many
weeks now before they could go about just
as they used to before they were ill.

There was only one drawback to the
pleasure of getting better: Malcolm, who
had been miserable when they were shut
up all the time in the hospital, now that
they were more like themselves, *would*
call them the "Misses Measles." Some-

times he forgot, and sometimes he did
not; but every little while they would hear
the obnoxious name, until the little girls
wished that their tormenting brother had
just had measles himself.

.

.

CHAPTER XIV.

A CHAPTER OF STORIES.

THE next day was not a very good day
in the hospital. Perhaps going down
to dinner had been too much for the little
patients, for they were rather cross, and
Clara even began to cry, saying that she
thought she was going to get well right
away, and now she was not getting well a
bit. Miss Harson neither scolded nor
preached sermons, but she took some
cold water and bathed each flushed face;
and when her two little charges felt more
comfortable, she wondered aloud if any one
cared to hear a story. For a moment there
was no answer, for Clara and Edie had been
very angry at Malcolm, who had called them
both "Miss Measles" when he came into
the ward, and Clara even passionately declared that she would never forgive him as
long as she lived. This was partly weak-

ness and nervousness, as her governess knew, and the mischievous boy was certainly very provoking; but Clara was easily teased, and, as Malcolm complained, "when she got mad she stayed mad such an awful long time." Edith had not said much, but she too felt cross, and Malcolm had called her a "cry-baby" when she shed tears over that ugly name. She thought that she was a poor little sick girl, and every one seemed very unkind to her.

"I have just found this little story in my portfolio," said Miss Harson, "and it is called

"THE STRAWBERRY-PICKERS.

"Two little Sunday-school girls, Sallie Hill and Tiny Blake, were out strawberrying together. Tiny Blake's name was really 'Clementina,' but this was too long for common, and she was so small of her age that 'Tiny' seemed to suit her very well. She was not handsomely clothed, for her parents were poor; but Sallie Hill, whose father kept the grocery-store, had a new dress every little while. This afternoon the dress was pink, and her round

straw hat had in it a bunch of artificial
roses. But I will not tell you more about
these little girls now, because you will find
out for yourselves by hearing them talk.

"Blossom Hill was a great place for wild
strawberries; they were small, to be sure,
beside the garden berries, but they were
such a bright red and had such a delicious
smell and taste that many people liked them
a great deal better. Besides, they could be
had just for the picking: no one had to pay
for them; and every garden does not have
in it a strawberry-bed.

" ' What is your mother going to do with
your berries, Tiny?' asked Sallie. 'We're
going to have strawberry-shortcake for
tea.'

" ' I guess we'll just eat 'em as they are,'
replied Tiny, with a little sigh at the idea of
strawberry-shortcake.

" ' Dear me!' said Sallie, with a toss of
her head; 'don't you ever have anything
good at your house?'

" ' Why, yes,' answered Tiny, rather
abashed at this rudeness, ' I think we have
a great deal that's good; and father read

to us one day about a little girl who thanked God because she had salt on her potatoes. We have butter, and milk too, with ours; so we have a great deal more than she had. Father says that most folks are not as thankful as they ought to be.'

"Sallie would probably have made some reply to this—perhaps not a very pleasant one—if she had not just then happened to see right before her a small spot where the strawberries grew so thick and red that she screamed out,

"'Oh, oh! What beauties!'

"Tiny came running up for a share of the berries, but Sallie, who was a square little personage, spread herself over them, saying,

"'You keep to your own place, Tiny Blake, and I'll keep to mine.'

"It seemed to Tiny that this sounded rather selfish; if she had found a nice spot, she would have called Sallie to share it with her. But she went off without a word, and presently her companion, who was picking as fast as she could, called out,

"'Do you remember your Sunday-school

verse, Tiny? Miss Green told us not to forget it through the week, you know. I remember mine: "All things whatsoever ye would that men should do to you, do ye even so to them." ' *

"Sallie was very proud of always knowing her lessons and of being one of Miss Green's best scholars, and she looked down on Tiny, who found it a trifle hard to remember things.

"'Oh yes,' said the little girl, after a moment's hesitation; 'now I know. This is my verse: "Blessed are the meek, for they"—they—"shall inherit the earth." That is it. And oh, Sallie, don't you recollect how beautifully Miss Green talked to us about it and told us what it meant to be "meek"? She said that to "inherit" a thing meant to have it because it belonged to you, and that when people were "meek," and didn't expect much, and didn't want things that others had, they got all the real good of 'em. And oh how I wish I could remember half she said! But I haven't a good memory like you.'

* Matt. vii. 12.

"It flashed suddenly upon Sallie that Tiny had something which she had not, and she began to see why it was that she always liked to be with her, although she did look down upon her.

"'And, Sallie,' Tiny continued, with a sweet smile, 'I don't think I mind a bit now about the strawberry-shortcake; I did at first.'

"How about the rule, 'Do unto others as ye would that they should do unto you'? Had Sallie so soon forgotten what Miss Green said about that?

"Very much to Tiny's surprise, a voice called out,

"'Tiny Blake, come straight over here and pick as many of these strawberries as you want. There's enough for both of us.'

"The two heads were soon bobbing sociably together, and the girls both enjoyed the last of the strawberry-picking best. They had such full baskets, too, to carry home, that every one was surprised.

"Somehow, Mrs. Hill made two short-cakes that afternoon, and the Blakes had

one of them for tea, although Tiny had
made up her mind that such things were
not for her. She enjoyed it, though, as
much as any of them."

"Wasn't Tiny sweet?" exclaimed Edith.
"She was such a dear little forgiving
thing !"

"Sallie was horrid," said Clara, "until
she got good."

"What seemed to change her?" asked
her governess.

"Why, I suppose it was Tiny's being so
meek and patient, wasn't it, Miss Harson ?"

Clara suddenly smiled and hid her face,
and Malcolm, who came in just at these
words, said with a wise air,

"That's worth remembering. Suppose
you try it, Clara? I mean Miss—"

But he didn't say "Measles;" he saw
something in his sister's face different from
usual, and was scarcely surprised when she
said sweetly,

"Forgive me, Malcolm, for being so cross
to you. I'll try not to be so again."

"You darling little sister !" exclaimed the

warm-hearted boy; "I knew all the time
that you didn't mean it. But I'm the
horrid one, and not you, for I'm a great
rude boy, and you're only a sick little girl.
Here's something I've made for you and
Edie; just finished it this morning."

A very pretty box for each little sister
was unfolded from soft tissue-paper, and
the lid and the sides had fine open-
work carving, which Malcolm had done
with his fret-saw. There were locks and
keys, too, and these, of course, made them
the more valuable. The invalids were
much surprised and pleased, and their
brother felt quite repaid for all his work
and trouble. As Miss Harson, too, admired the boxes, he resolved immediately
to set about making one for her.

"That must have been a story that was
just getting finished when I came in," said
Malcolm, after his gifts had been duly admired, "but I dare say it was a very short
one. Don't you think you could find another one, Miss Harson, about boys?"

"I certainly can," replied his governess,
laughingly, "and I think you deserve it,

after the work you have done. There is only one boy, though, in my story; do you think you can be satisfied with that?"

Malcolm obligingly promised to try, and Miss Harson continued:

"The boy in this story is an historical character and a great favorite of mine; his life more beautifully teaches the great lesson of forgiveness of injuries than almost anything I have ever known. I cannot do better, I think, than to call his story

'THE GREAT VICTORY.

"One day in the year 943 a little boy only eight years old took part in two solemn services in the French city of Rouen. The first was the funeral of his father, the great and good duke William of Normandy, who had been basely murdered by his enemy, the count of Flanders; the second was his own coronation as his father's successor.

"Dearly had the boy's father loved him, and dearly was the father loved in return; but the bewildered lad was taken directly

15

from the funeral in the grand cathedral to the church, where he received the ducal robe and coronet.   His father and the good abbot who had been his friend and counselor had taught him to pray, and now, overcome with grief and the solemn oath he had taken to be 'the good and true ruler of his people,' he whispered softly, 'O God my Father, help me to keep it!'   The day before, when gazing on his murdered father, he had almost uttered a dreadful vow that as soon as his arm was strong enough he would avenge his death on the wicked count of Flanders, but his rash words were interrupted by the good abbot, whose solemn reproach brought a shower of tears from the flashing blue eyes of the young duke. Amid his sobs Richard had asked his friend and guide if it could be right to let that cruel traitor go unpunished, while his noble father lay there, struck down by his murderous hand.

"'Yes,' Abbot Martin replied; 'in his own good time the Lord will punish Arnulf of Flanders for his crime, but the

son of the murdered duke of Normandy
is the very one who shall show him love
and mercy in his day of need.'

"The words sounded strangely in the
boy's bitter sorrow, but had not his dear
father himself made him promise, the last
time he saw him living, that if he should
fall in some contest he would not revenge
him except by forgiving his enemy? But
how could he do it? the boy thought as
his tears fell fast; how could he do it?
And yet on the cross his Redeemer
prayed for his murderers. He earnestly
wished to do right, but as he was only a
weak, sorrowful little boy, and more wearied with his heavy robe and his coronet,
and with the long train of nobles who
knelt in turn to kiss his hand as their
liege-lord, than pleased with the honor
done him, he murmured at the close of
that long day, 'I am very, very tired of
being duke of Normandy.'

"Kind friends and vassals were devoted
to the little duke, who was a bright, fearless and most lovable boy; but the different provinces of France were in a

state of continual strife, and wicked men tried to make a prisoner of Richard that they might get possession of his dukedom of Normandy. The king of France was the most powerful of these enemies, and by fair words and a great show of affection for him he got the boy into his palace, where he had promised him playmates in his two sons. But, once in his power, the king treated him with coldness and neglect, and the queen was even more unkind. As for the two princes, Lothaire, who was about Richard's age, was a cruel, domineering boy with whom he could have no companionship, and the younger one, Carloman, was a weak, timid little fellow over whom his brother tyrannized. He soon, however, came to love Richard, who was always kind and gentle to him, and the two were constant companions and playmates. It was a dreary life for the little duke of Normandy, who was really a prisoner, but he had with him two faithful attendants who were ready to defend him with their lives.

"At last, when the king was away on a

journey, the boy fell sick, and his friends suspected that the food sent to him had been poisoned; for in those days this was a common way of getting rid of a person whose death was desired for any reason. The wicked king was supposed to have gone away on purpose, and to have left directions that Richard should be put out of the way during his absence. It was quite time to get him out of the palace by some means; so his faithful squire, Osmond, rolled him in a bundle of straw and then carried it out to the stable, as though he had been going to feed his horse. They got off safely, and after a weary journey the young duke, nearly dead with sickness and fatigue, found himself once more in his own domain and surrounded by loving faces. He soon got well again, but he was moved about for safety from one castle to another while his friends were fighting for him against his enemies.

"At length came news of a great victory, and the king of France was taken prisoner. But after a time he was allowed to return to his kingdom by placing his two sons in the hands of the Normans until he could pay his ransom. They were brought to the castle of Bayeux, and it seemed a fine opportunity for Richard to triumph over the evil Lothaire, who had made him suffer so much when he was at the court of France, but, instead of this, he was gentle and courteous to the ill-behaved prince and most loving to the poor little sickly Carloman, whom he had led to the Saviour. The little duke of Normandy was practicing the beautiful lesson of forgiveness, and he had his reward. Carloman died while with him with words of hope and trust on his lips, and even Lothaire, who was restored to his parents at Richard's intercession, was touched by Richard's generosity, and said that he never would forget what he had done for him.

"Years passed, and the little duke had become a strong and noble man. The count of Flanders had made many treacherous attempts to get possession of Normandy, and three times he had tried to assassinate Richard. At last, bent and feeble with age, he fled for his life from the French and Normans, who had all vowed to kill him for the wrongs inflicted on the duke. In his wanderings he came unexpectedly upon the man whom he had so deeply injured, and, overcome with terror, he fell at his feet praying for mercy. 'Richard the Fearless,' as he was everywhere called, who was afraid of nothing but to do wrong, forgave even this enemy and ministered to his wants.

"'Vengeance is mine: I will repay, saith the Lord.'"

"That was a splendid fellow," said Malcolm, thoughtfully. "I'd like to be a duke."

"It was not being a duke that made him the man he was," replied his governess, "but being a Christian; remember that, Malcolm. 'Richard the Fearless' was a noble specimen of a true Christian gentleman, and he would have been that had he been born in a peasant's hut instead of in a ducal castle. Malcolm Kyle can never be duke of Normandy, yet he can have what this duke valued far more highly than he valued his dukedom."

CHAPTER XV.

JANEY.

ONE morning Dr. Gates brought a little visitor to spend the day. She was not a surprise as the kittens were, for Miss Harson had been thinking of it for some time, and, having asked the good doctor if it were quite safe for the little girl, she told Clara and Edith that if they would like to have her Janey Purse could come and spend the day with them. They did like it, very much; for, besides the pleasure of having a visitor, they were quite curious on the subject of Janey, who seemed to them entirely different from any children they had ever known, being more like a grown-up woman cut very short. She was only nine years old, but she was the eldest of four children, and she knew more of work, poor child! than she did of play. Mrs. Purse was not afraid of her catching

the measles by visiting the little invalids, for
Dr. Gates said there was no danger now;
and, as the little Purses had had a variety
of diseases when they lived in that wretched
tenement in New York, their mother seemed
to think that measles might have been among
them without her knowing particularly
about it. So Janey, a very pale, quiet-
looking little person, was set down by Dr.
Gates at Elmridge at about eleven o'clock
in the morning, and she was to be taken
back when the carriage went to the station
for Mr. Kyle. She felt quite important,
though a little frightened, at the idea of
visiting at the great house, but she had
fallen in love with the sweet young lady
when she was sick, and she liked the looks
of the pretty little girls whom she had seen
on their sleighride. The last thing her
mother had told her was to "remember
her manners," and poor Janey was sometimes puzzled to know just what they
were.

Miss Harson had said something of the
same kind to her little charges, but in a
different way. Janey had been sent for,

she told them, not only to amuse them, but to give the visitor herself a pleasure, as this was a thing she seldom had, and they must try to make her enjoy her visit not only because it was right, but because this was the most certain way of enjoying it themselves. Clara and Edith both assured their governess that they were so glad to see a little girl again they would do their best to make her happy, and even Malcolm, who had seen Janey when she was sick, declared that she was a nice little thing and he did not at all mind her coming.

When Janey appeared at the door of the hospital, she said, "Oh!" and then stood quite still. It seemed like heaven, she told her mother afterward, the beautiful room with its flowers and birds and sunshine, the glowing fire and bright furnishings, the pictures and texts, and the Good Shepherd with the lambs, and through all the delicious smell of the hyacinths and the mignonette.

Clara and Edith were sitting in their little rockers beside the table in the middle of the room, busy with their needles and sur-

rounded by bits of silk and other finery
that seemed very magnificent to little
Janey. But there was another rocker by
the table, for the visitor, and Miss Harson and the little girls came forward and
spoke so kindly that Janey soon found herself fairly in the room without seeming to
remember how she got there.

"This is our hospital," said the young
lady; "for you know we have had two
sick little girls here for quite a long time,
and we have tried to make it as pleasant
as we could for them. Do you like it?"

"I wouldn't ever want to leave it," replied
Janey, breathlessly, when at last she found
courage to speak.

"Oh yes, you would," said Clara, "for it
isn't a bit nice to be sick, and we want to
get out to walk and play as we used to."

"Are you ever sick, Janey?" asked Edith,
softly.

"Yes," whispered Janey, for she was too
shy to talk much; but she looked admiringly at Edie, who had, she thought, the
loveliest eyes she had ever seen. They
were pretty eyes, but it was the love and

the sympathy shining through them that now made them seem so beautiful.

"Don't you remember, dear," said Miss Harson, "the little sick girl at Mrs. Purse's when Malcolm and I went there? It was Janey, who looks very much better now than I ever expected her to look."—"But none too well," added the young lady to herself as she glanced at the pale little face that looked up at her with a sweet smile.—"Come," she continued, taking the little hand in hers; "let us first go through the ward and visit all the patients."

Clara and Edith laughed at the little visitor's puzzled face, and she soon joined in the laugh herself when she saw all the dolls in their beds, as though they had been real patients.

"They are going soon to a genuine hospital," said Edith—"as soon as they are well enough to be moved."

Janey looked more surprised than ever, and Miss Harson said, with her pleasant smile,

"You will think us very queer people here at Elmridge because we make believe so much. This is our make-believe hospital, and the dolls are make-believe patients, but they are going to a real hospital, where we hope they will amuse some really sick children. Were you ever in a hospital, Janey?"

"Yes, ma'am," replied the low voice, "mother took me to see father when he was hurt. He died there."

"Oh, you poor little Janey!" exclaimed Edie, impulsively; "I am so sorry for you!"

There were no tears, though, on Janey's patient face; she only looked a little more sad. There had been so many things in her short recollection to cry over! Miss Harson felt the little hand clasp hers more closely; that was all.

The child lingered a long time over the flowers, and touched one or two caressingly, as if they had been living things: she said that they made her feel happy; but the picture of the Good Shepherd held her longest.

"Where did you learn about him, Janey?" asked Miss Harson.

"At the mission school, ma'am, where I

used to go in New York. Our teacher was a very kind lady and came to see us. I guess it's easy to be good with such nice things around."

"Is it, Clara?" asked her governess; for the two little sisters were looking very rosy after Janey said this.

"No," was the truthful reply, "not easy at all, and we are often very naughty; but we try."

"That is what we must all keep doing as long as we live," continued Miss Harson, "and you will find, Janey, that it is not easy for any one, rich or poor, to be 'good.' But God has promised to help with his Holy Spirit those who really strive to please him, and the youngest child who seeks him in prayer is as near to him as the greatest king can be."

The little girl looked as though this were wonderful news, and she seemed to be drinking in every word that was said to her. Presently the young lady stooped down and kissed her, and then left her for a while to Clara and Edith.

"Come and see what we are doing,"

said Clara, hospitably; "we work now for an hour every morning, and Miss Harson shows us how to do ever so many pretty things. We are making little pincushions for the sick children; this one shaped like a pansy is for the Heart's-Ease Cot."

"What's the Heart's-Ease Cot?" asked Janey, with very wide eyes; and she would have added, "What's all the rest of it?" only she was afraid this would not be "remembering her manners."

Everything was explained by degrees, and then the little visitor was made very happy by being allowed to help by sticking pins all around the edge of each finished pincushion. She too wanted to do something for the sick children, she said.

"What do you do every day at home, Janey?" asked her little hostesses. "Do you sew?"

No; Janey did not sew. Mother said that when she tried her fingers were all thumbs.

"How very funny!" exclaimed Edith, looking very hard at the fingers. "And do they change back again?"

Janey laughed for the first time since her arrival, and then she explained that, as nobody could sew with thumbs only, her mother meant that her fingers were not of much more use than so many thumbs.

"But there are lots of other things to do," she continued, "now that mother has more work; and I'm the oldest, you know, and she says that she quite depends on me. I make up all the beds"—there were only two of them—"and kindle the fire, and wash dishes, and sweep up, and mind the baby, and go of errands. I guess there's more, too, but I can't think of 'em all now."

"When do you go to school?" asked Clara; for there seemed to be no room for school among these duties.

Janey said that she did not go at all, and her little companions pitied her very much when they found that she could not read. The little girl herself seemed to take this quite as a matter of course, yet she thought it would be nice to know what was inside of those pretty books on the shelf.

The trio were so busy talking and working that when Miss Harson and Jane came in to arrange the dinner the girls were surprised to find it so late. Janey quietly watched the preparations, thinking that she had never seen anything so beautiful in her life before; and when they sat down at the prettily-laid table, she was lost in admiration of the glass and china and the flowers in the centre, to say nothing of the dainty dishes which Kitty had sent up for "her young ladies." Janey behaved quite like a little lady herself, and she looked like one, too, in a nice plaid dress which Clara had outgrown, and in her neat collar and with smoothly-brushed hair. When, with a little girl on each side of her, Miss Harson stood to say grace before dinner, it was something quite new to the visitor; but she too bowed her head reverently, as though she understood that this bountiful meal was the direct gift of her heavenly Father. The child would have liked to take her own share home to her mother, but "remembering her manners" kept her from speaking of it.

After dinner the children were turned

16

into the hall to play, and a merry time they had of it with "Puss-in-the-Corner," "Blindman's-Buff," and everything that could be thought of. Miss Harson and Malcolm joined them slyly in "Blindman's-Buff," and very much astonished and rather frightened was Janey to find that she had "caught" the young gentleman. They laughed and shouted with delight, and, as Kitty said, "racketed around" until they were fairly tired out. Then they went back to the hospital, where Jane had cleared away the dinner-things and let in fresh air and trimmed the fire, until it was as sweet and bright as possible; and Janey thought again that she would never want to leave it. She thought so still more when she saw the lovely work that was spread out on the table. First there were large newspapers, to catch the droppings and scraps, and on these were two or three books made of leaves of colored muslin, a quantity of colored pictures and small engravings which had been cut from books and papers, a bowl of paste, brushes and some white rags. This all looked so delightful

that the little visitor breathlessly waited
to see what was to be done.

"Can't Janey cut out some pictures?"
asked Clara as Miss Harson was seating
them at the table.

"Certainly she can," was the reply.—
"Here is a seat for you, Janey, and here
are scissors. Cut any of the pictures that
you like out of these books, and trim them
off neatly in this way."

The little girl was quick to learn, because she attended closely to what was
said to her, and Miss Harson was quite
surprised to see how nicely she did her
work. She enjoyed it so much, too, that
it was a pleasure to watch her. She made
a very good selection of pictures, and the
young lady brought another book for her
to paste them in.

"Will these be your very own?" asked
Janey, admiring the beautiful scrapbooks
which her companions would soon have
finished.

"No, indeed!" They laughed, as if the
idea had been a very funny one. "They
are to be sent to the hospital to amuse the

sick children. That was what made it so pleasant to do them."

Miss Harson saw the little face light up at this reply, and she said,

"Would you like, dear, to make a scrap-book for some little girl who has no nice playthings?"

Janey looked very shy at this question, for she was afraid that she could not do it well; but she fairly blushed with delight as she whispered, "Yes, ma'am." The young lady saw there was not a thought of self, yet, except for the children's Christmas gifts, she certainly had "no nice playthings." The child was only thinking how delightful it was to be taught such pretty work by "her beautiful Miss Harson"—what would Clara and Edith have said to that **pronoun**?—and how, if she did it nicely, some little girl would be very glad to get the scrapbook. So she cut and pasted with the utmost patience, and was rewarded by Miss Harson's praise of her work, which really deserved praise for its neatness.

"And you like that picture very much, Janey?" asked the young lady as she saw the little visitor's eyes resting on "The Good Shepherd" very frequently.

"Yes," replied Janey, as though half afraid to say it; "he looks right at me so kind of loving."

"The Good Shepherd is indeed 'loving,' dear—so full of love that he gave his life for the sheep. But I must read you a story which I found to-day among some papers, because, strangely enough, it is called 'Janie's Picture,' and it is also about the blessed Saviour."

"Then *you* didn't write it, Miss Harson?" asked Clara, in a tone tinged with disappointment.

"No, dear, I did not write this story," was the smiling reply; "but I wish that I had written it, if that will comfort you, for it is full of sweetness. We will leave the pasting now for to-day, as by the time I have finished reading Thomas will probably be ready to take Janey home."

Everything was stopped the moment Miss Harson spoke, and Malcolm had contrived to join the group just as the young lady began to read the story of

JANIE'S PICTURE.

The bells were ringing merrily through the clear, frosty air over snow piled high in the street; the sleighs dashed gayly on with their merry occupants; the lights shone out clearly from the shop-windows, and people passed hurriedly to and fro on their way to their homes, some with happy, some with expectant, but some with anxious, faces, even on that night of all other nights of the year when the heart should be joyous because it is Christmas eve.

Yet, of all the faces of the passers by, there is not one so anxious as that of a child who is stationed on tip-toe before a large shop-window, peering inside at all the light and brightness as she stands half in shadow in the cold outside. The snow is on her golden hair and her little hands are purple with the cold, but, nevertheless, she stands there all unconscious, her thoughts intent on what she sees inside in that gleaming light. Her eyes grow larger and more wistful as she gazes, her forehead pressed against the window-pane, at a beautiful picture on the other side. It was one of

"Christ Blessing Little Children," and it
was so distinct that the hot Eastern sun
seemed to blaze down on the low roofs of
the houses, while a group of palm trees in
the centre flung their shadows on the
ground beneath. Under these the figure
of Christ was seated, his head slightly
raised and his face bearing a tender look
as he stretched out his arms to the children
who were gathering about him. There was
so much of gentleness in it that the hard
lines in the child's own face, caused by cold
and want, seemed to soften as she looked.

"What you lookin' at, Janie?" asked a
voice behind her; and the little girl looked
up, to see Tim the bootblack standing beside her.

Tim lived in the same alley, almost next
door, and was a good-natured fellow, although somewhat rough at times; but
Janie liked him and looked up to him
as a marvel of learning, for he had been
to school once, ever so long ago, for two
quarters.

"I'm lookin' at that picture inside, Tim,
of the man with the little children. Ain't

he got a kind face? Tim," she added, with great seriousness, "do you really think he is alive somewhere, and that we could find him? Them children in the picture seems to be kind of ragged and poor-like, yet he don't seem to mind their rags. Tim, you can read; can't you make out them words at the bottom, all in gold?"

Tim scratched his head thoughtfully, but after much puzzling and hesitation he finally made out the text: "Suffer the little children to come unto me, and forbid them not; for of such is the kingdom of heaven."

"There, now!" said Janie, quite triumphantly; "I knowed he was a-sayin' something just like that. 'For of such is the kingdom of heaven,'" she added, thoughtfully. A moment later she looked up, her eyes full of tears: "We've no need to look further, Tim. I was just a-goin' to say as how we'd go an' look fur him, but them children, though they're all ragged and has got very little clothes to keep 'em warm, belongs to the kingdom of heaven—wherever that may be. And it's away far off, in a strange kind of land, and we can't git there. Tim, you knows everythin'; you don't think we can git there, do you?"

"I dunno," replied Tim, gruffly. "I heard of it a great while ago, but I've forgotten mostly of what were said. There be no good, though, a-searchin' for the man in the picture, Janie, for he died years an' years ago."

Once more the eyes turned toward the bright lights and the little face rested against the window-pane, but there were tears streaming down the pale cheeks now. There sat the man with the tender look on his face and his kind arms stretched out toward the little children, while he held the youngest and weakest on his knee.

"And I thought he was alive an' I could find him!" said little Janie, with a sob.

"Oh, you've no call to fret now, Janie," said Tim, good-naturedly. "Come, run away now; it's time you was to home, an' I wish you a Merry Christmas."

"What's that, Tim?"

"Oh, I dunno," he answered, with some

impatience. "For a young un, you ask a heap o' questions."

Janie turned away sadly. She was still thinking of her disappointment.

"'Merry Christmas'!" she repeated to herself; "I dunno what the last means, but I know the first, and little cause *I* have to be merry, when I ain't tasted a crust o' bread sence mornin'. I wouldn't care much, though, if I could be one o' them children hangin' round the man in the picture. But then he ain't alive now; Tim said he were dead."

Still that kind face came before the poor girl, and those arms were stretched out to her. There were no other children gathered around; the arms seemed stretched to her alone, while the lips appeared to utter the words, "Suffer the little children to come unto me, and forbid them not."

So all-absorbed in these thoughts on the street-crossing where she stood was Janie that she did not see nor hear a heavy cart come rattling down the street, the horses bounding on and their driver all unconscious, until suddenly his vehicle passed

over something, and one long moan told
him only too plainly what that something
was. But after a moment's pain the poor
little waif sank into a deep swoon, the vis-
ion of that gentle face, those outstretched
arms, the last sight of which she was conscious. They lifted her up, crushed and
wounded, from off the snow, and carried
her to the hospital; and those who
watched beside her through that night
wondered at some of the broken sen-
tences she uttered in her delirious state:

"'He's not alive, he's dead,' Tim said.
But he *is* alive," she would add; "I saw
him only a little while ago, with his arms
stretched out to me, and now—now they're
gone. He's gone!"

The sun rose with such a bright golden
smile that next morning it made the snow
and the ice glitter on roof and on tree, and
in the streets the joy-bells pealed from out
the church-towers of the great city, for it
was the birthday of the King of kings.
Then, for the first time, the blue eyes
unclosed, and the child came back to consciousness to find herself lying in a white

bed with a kind nurse beside her, and there—oh joy!—hanging right before her, on the opposite wall, lightened by the sun's morning kiss, the picture which she had learned to love, that face still gazing down into her own and those arms still outstretched for her. Then, with all the strength in her poor tired little body, she stretched out her own arms and said, her eyes bright with a glad surprise,

"You are still there! You are so good; you haven't gone away!"

It was a long time before little Janie rose from her bed, and almost six months before she could leave the hospital; but she always looked back upon those days as the happiest of her life, because she learned that what Tim had said in his ignorance was not true—that, although the "man in the picture," whom she had unconsciously learned to love, had died so many years ago, he died to rise again and live for evermore; and she there had felt the closer embrace of his divine arms stretched out no less to her than to the children of old.

"What did she do when she got well?" asked Janey, eagerly. "Did she go to live in the country?"

"I do not know, dear," replied Miss Harson, smiling at the question; "the story does not tell us anything more about her. But she had found her Saviour, and we may be very sure that, wherever she was, she was happy."

The children all liked the story, and their visitor said it was "the beautifullest one she had ever heard."

CHAPTER XVI.

DOING GOOD.

WHEN Janey was taken home by Thomas, with many lingering looks at the beautiful house where she had spent such a pleasant day, a basket of provisions went with her, and some fine sewing for Mrs. Purse to do at her leisure. The good woman felt very grateful to her kind friend Miss Harson, and to the young ladies at Elmridge, for giving her little girl such a delightful visit. Janey had something to talk about now, she said, for a month to come.

But it was not long before Janey had other wonderful things to talk about.

"Only think, Miss Harson!" exclaimed Clara, when their visitor was fairly out of hearing; "Janey can't read a bit, and she's nine years old. She doesn't even know her letters."

"Well, dear," was the reply, "what are you going to do about it?"

What *was* Clara going to do? Why, she had not thought of doing anything except to be surprised; but presently she saw something to do, and asked eagerly,

"Oh, Miss Harson, could she come here for me to teach her?"

"I see no objection to it," replied her governess, "if you are quite in earnest and willing to persevere even when it seems like a disagreeable task. But once begun, remember, the lessons must be continued. I think that an hour on Wednesday and Saturday afternoons will do very nicely."

Clara was all enthusiasm and ready to promise anything, and even wished to have Janey for an hour every day that she might sooner learn to read; but Miss Harson was quite sure that twice a week would be enough for both teacher and pupil.

The good work was begun, and went on very pleasantly, Janey being as anxious to learn as Clara was to teach; and the alphabet-blocks which had been stored away

when Edie outgrew them were brought
to light again, and proved a great help.
The little scholar was industrious and per-
severing, and Clara so much enjoyed what
she called "doing something for somebody" that she was always faithful to her
hour and interested in Janey's progress.

Miss Harson was glad to find her ex-
periment with Janey had succeeded so
well, and that, besides being benefited herself, she was really doing her little companions a great deal of good. They did
not act foolishly by spoiling Janey with too
much kindness, and Clara was learning a
lesson of patience in teaching a very ig-
norant pupil, while Edith was learning self-
denial in being willing to be put aside for
Janey's improvement.

Janey took a great interest in the hospital from hearing Clara and Edith talk
so much about it; she was very much
pleased when, after taking her first lesson,
Miss Harson said that she would read a
story she had written lately in which there
was something about the hospital.

"And about a little girl who went to the

seashore because she had been ill," the young lady added, smilingly, to two other little girls who had been ill, and who took so long to get strong again that Dr. Gates and papa were talking seriously about having them go to the seashore as soon as the warm weather came.

"Oh, good, good!" exclaimed both Clara and Edith, with a great deal more interest than ever.

But Janey was not going to the seashore, and she did not quite see what there was so particularly "good" in that. She was just as eager for the story, though, and she scarcely took her eyes from Miss Harson whilst that lady read

DAISY AND DELY.

It was a very close, showery day in the early part of August—the kind of day that every one speaks of as "disagreeable;" but Daisy Hinton was so happy that morning that she did not think about the weather at all. She was quite a pale, thin little Daisy, for she had been very ill during most of those long beautiful summer days which

17

had slipped away somehow until there was not much of summer left; and Daisy and Daisy's mamma had stayed in the hot city waiting until the doctor said that salt air was all that his little patient needed now. And, of all delightful things, they were going to the seashore where Aunt Clara and the twins had been staying for ever so long.

Daisy was getting so impatient on the journey that she declared she should certainly fly if the boat and the cars did not go faster. Mamma thought that they were going pretty fast now, but they had to stop once and make a change, and then Daisy was just ready to cry. Suppose that, after all, they should be left by the train? It was too dreadful to think of! And there mamma was actually stopping and talking to some one right on the way to the boat!

"Oh, mamma!" exclaimed the little girl, in great excitement; "do come!"

Perhaps it was the sight of another child, two or three years older than herself, crying bitterly, that kept back Daisy's tears, and it did seem to her that never in all her short life had she seen any one cry so.

Mrs. Hinton was trying to find out what was the matter, and the girl was trying to tell her, but she could not seem to stop crying long enough to do it. All the time she held tightly by the hand a pale little mite of a child much paler and thinner than Daisy. This child did not look strong enough even to cry, but the blue lips had such a pitiful expression, and the little wan face was so pinched that it was sad to see.

The big girl—who was not so very big, after all—at last told how she had lost the few pennies that were to take them over the ferry, and now they could not get home to their mother, who would be dreadfully worried about them.

"And where have you been?" asked the lady, kindly.

Mary Ann—for that, she said, was her name, Mary Ann Jacobs—managed to sob out, "Seaside Home; all along of Dely, here," and then Mrs. Hinton knew all.

Mary Ann was quite sturdy-looking, and her light hair was in two tight little braids, while Dely's, of darker brown, was cut close to her head.

"And what is the matter with Dely?" continued Mrs. Hinton.

"It's her hip, ma'am, the doctor says; and sometimes she does be real bad with it."

"Poor little thing!" said the kind lady. "But I think I know of a place where she can be made better, and you must tell me where you live, so that when I return to the city I can see about getting her there."

Mary Ann told Mrs. Hinton the street and the number, and then Mrs. Hinton put some money in the girl's hand to pay the ferryman and the car-fare on the other side; and, telling her not to lose it and to be very careful of Dely, she hurried on with Daisy, just in time for the last boat. But her little daughter was not impatient now; and when Mrs. Hinton said, "Are you sorry, dear, that we stopped a few moments?" Daisy's face looked very red and sorrowful.

"No, indeed, mamma," she replied, earnestly; "and I do hope that poor dear little Dely can be made well again. Isn't the hospital the place where you are going to send her? And can't she have my own little Heart's-Ease Cot?"

"We will see, dear," replied mamma, "and as soon as we are settled at Long Beach I will write to Sister Julia about little Dely."

Daisy had what she called "a most elegant time" with her twin-cousins at the seashore, and the pale little girl soon became as brown as a berry and raced and shouted with the merriest of them all; but she did not forget Mary Ann and Dely, and she talked about them to every one she knew, until her mother declared that every one would be tired of hearing the same story. But one lady after another handed Mrs. Hinton a crisp bill to be used "for the poor little sick child," until there was more money than Mrs. Jacobs had ever seen at once before, and little Dely had many comforts to which she had been a stranger.

When Daisy really saw the little girl in the Heart's-Ease Cot, she declared herself "too happy for anything;" and although the kind doctor said that she could never be a well, strong child, he thought she could be made much more comfortable. She was already so much so that, except for leaving her mother and Mary Ann, Dely was almost willing to be sick for the sake of being permitted to stay at the hospital.

"I'm so glad!" said Janey, when the story was finished.

"Glad of what, dear?" asked Miss Harson.

"For the little sick girl who got better at that nice hospital," was the reply.

To Clara and Edith this story was particularly charming because the people in it went to the seashore, and that night they dreamed that they had started with Miss Harson, who stopped to speak with some one and got left by the train. Or, rather, Clara dreamed it, and spoke of it the next morning, when Edie, who had a confused notion of having dreamed something, declared that that was it.

CHAPTER XVII.

WHAT THE FLOWERS TAUGHT.

MALCOLM had been particularly thoughtful in devising various pleasures for his invalid sisters, whom he heartily wished well again, in spite of the many attractions of the "hospital;" and one bleak day in March he appeared with a flower-pot containing a white lily that was warranted to bloom in a reasonable time. Having deposited his burden, he went back for one exactly like it, and then presented the plants, with a comical speech, . to Clara and Edith. "These tokens of my esteem," as he magniloquently called them, had been begged from John, who from some inexplicable reason was not anxious to part with them; but the covering of the flower-pots was Malcolm's own design, and he was not a little proud of it.   He had bought the common covers made in fine slats of wood and gilded them; then, with Miss Harson's help, he hung a fringe of small cones, also gilded, around the top of each pot.   The effect was really handsome, and the little girls were greatly pleased with their present.   It seemed as if lilies with any sense of gratitude must bloom finely in such gorgeous residences, and so in the end these lilies did.   Clara and Edith appeared to think them even more entirely their own than were the hyacinths which their governess had so kindly planted for them, and they watched and watered their charges every day with jealous care.

Of course the lilies were displayed to Janey, and, as Miss Harson noticed the little girl's face while she gazed wistfully at the plants, she slipped quietly out to the greenhouse to see if John could be bribed into parting with another of his treasures.

"I wouldn't do it for any one else, ma'am," said the worthy gardener, who evidently thought that he owned the greenhouse, if not the whole place, "but as it's yerself, and the little one, you say, can learn a great deal from the plant if she has it to care for, why here's another lily I can let her have."

It was a plain red pot, to be sure, but what did that matter, when there was such a lovely plant in it? Besides, one of those gilded affairs like Clara's and Edith's would have looked rather out of place in the shabby little room where the lily was to grow and blossom. So Janey, who had not expected anything of the kind—only thinking for a moment how lovely it would be to have a plant of her very own, and how good she would be to it if she could have one—found her wildest wish suddenly granted. In her exuberance of gratitude she threw her arms around Miss Harson and kissed her. Then, rather frightened at what she had done, she stood looking upon her gift with a crimson face, until the voice that seemed to her the sweetest in the world said kindly,

"I am glad you like it so much, dear."

Then Miss Harson told the children all

about this beautiful calla-lily—how it grows in the pools and on the river-edges of Africa, and therefore requires heat and a great deal of water, and that, also, like other plants, it needs air as human beings do.

For several days the plant flourished nicely, but one unfortunate morning little Mamie, who was but three years old, cut off the entire top of glossy leaves and walked up to Janey with it, saying, "Put water." She had seen her sister do this with the flowers and the leaves which she occasionally brought from Elmridge, and the little one took a notion that it would be a good thing for the calla-lily.

Poor Janey's disappointment was so great that she raised her hand quickly for the bestowal of a blow, but the mischievous little offender stood close beside her, so smiling and unconscious that Janey felt instantly ashamed of her anger, and instead of striking the child she burst into tears. Mamie softly stroked her face and asked if she was sick, while Mrs. Purse hurried in from the next room to see what was the matter. The bunch of leaves in

the little fat hand and the knife lying beside the cropped plant at once told the
story, and Mamie was snatched up for
punishment. But Janey pleaded so earnestly with her mother not to punish the
child that she was released ; and, sticking
the leaves in the pot as well as she could,
the little one said triumphantly,

"There! all right now."

Janey smiled sadly ; there was an end,
she thought, to her beautiful plant and its
expected blossoms. It was her dear Miss
Harson's gift, too. and this made the loss
harder to bear. Great was her surprise,
then, when the young lady said,

"The plant is not dead, dear, although
it seems so now ; it will live again, like our
bodies when they are put into the grave
to await the resurrection. And that poor
broken calla will teach a better lesson than
if it had bloomed. You will have no blossoms from it this season, Janey, but with
proper care during the summer and the
autumn it will reward you with flowers on
some of the first cold days, although now
it shows no sign of leaf or of flower."

The next comforting thing was a story, and this too was forthcoming. Miss Harson said that Janey would probably particularly like this one because it was about a little girl whose flowers were spoiled, and the name of the story was

DAISIES AND LILIES.

Sadie Clay was a sweet little girl with a face that seemed to peep forth from her blue worsted school-hood like a spring flower. Every one liked Sadie, she was so bright and full of life, and yet so careful never to do or to say a rude or an unkind thing.

Mr. Mervale, the clergyman at Long Pond, where Sadie lived, did a great many pleasant things to interest the children, and one Sunday in early winter, in speaking of their spring anniversary, when the church was always dressed with flowers, he told them that he had a new plan for this. Flowers, he said, were always a sweeter and a truer offering when they had been carefully tended by loving hands, whether they were intended to give pleasure to others or to express gratitude to God for his goodness and loving-kindness toward us; and some poor servant of his, or even a little child, could raise a flower that would send up to heaven far sweeter incense than the richest perfume from the wreaths and bouquets that were bought at the florist's. Of course there was a great deal of talking as the children walked home from Sunday-school that afternoon, and before separating most of them had selected the flowers they meant to cultivate, and white roses, callas and hyacinths were soon appropriated.

Sadie Clay, who was always modest about putting herself forward, began to fear that there would be nothing left for her. Suddenly, however, she happened to think of white daisies. But she did not quite see where they were to come from at this season of the year. Sadie, however, had great faith in her father; he always in his quiet way managed to get her all she asked for.

The Clays lived in a very pleasant, comfortable-looking farmhouse that stood some distance back from the gate and had a porch of trellis-work covered over with evergreen

and honeysuckle. Sadie and her brother
Reuben went skipping up the walk, and
their father appeared in the doorway to
meet them.

"Oh, father," exclaimed the little girl,
' can I have some white daisies? I want
'em for the Sunday-school anniversary."

Mr. Clay was not much of a talker, and
first he took Sadie up in his arms and kissed her, then whispered something in her ear.

"*I* know something," said she, looking
mischievously at Reuben.

"I hope you do," he replied, in a dignified
way, as he strode off to the sitting-room.

Sadie laughed again as she said, "Oh,
father, you're *so* funny!" but she felt sure
that the daisies were really coming.

What Mr. Clay whispered to his little
daughter was this: "If you see a cherry-
colored cat to-morrow afternoon, I think
you'll see the daisies."

" Who ever heard of a red cat?" thought
Sadie; but, as her father did not say that
she would not see the daisies without the
cat, she went to bed full of hope.

The next day, soon after breakfast, Mr.

Clay got the wagon ready and drove off to the county-town. He often had business there, and one of his errands now was to find a box of white daisies warranted to bloom at the desired time.

Sadie watched her father sharply when he returned, late in the afternoon, but he drove directly to the barn; and when he finally appeared again—how long it seemed! —he had something covered in one hand, and Sally, their old black cat, in the other.

"Here's your cherry-colored cat," said he, "and here's— Something else."

For a moment Sadie was too much astonished even to uncover the "something else," but presently the brown paper was lifted, and there were the daisies—or, rather, there were the plants and the leaves, for blossoms were yet to come.

"Oh, father," cried the happy little girl as she gave him a hug, "you're *so* good!"

It was just two weeks from the anniversary, and buds had actually appeared on the daisies. Sadie's delight was intense, and one day, when the white of the blossoms could plainly be seen, she went with her mother to visit a poor consumptive woman who lived quite near. Mrs. Smith looked very pale, but she had a chubby little boy about two years old whose cheeks seemed just bursting with fatness.

"Is there anything you would like to have?" asked Mrs. Clay as she rose to go.

"I have plenty to eat and to drink, thank you," replied the sick woman, "and it may be wrong in me to say anything, for I know I'm more comfortable than I deserve to be; but I sometimes think, as I lie here, if I only had a flower to look at—a *growing* flower, I mean; something to remind me of the spring when it looks so cold and dreary outside—I'd feel better."

"You shall have my daisies," exclaimed Sadie, impulsively; "I've got some beautiful ones just coming out. I'm 'tending 'em, you know, for our Sunday-school anniversary, but you can have 'em to look at till then."

Mrs. Smith was so grateful that Sadie thought of little else but her pleasure.

"I do not believe they'll do so well

there," said her mother, on their way home;
" I'm afraid you were rather thoughtless,
Sadie dear, in promising them to Mrs.
Smith."

" I guess they will," replied Sadie, hope-
fully; "and, anyhow, I couldn't help it,
mother. She looked so sick, and perhaps
she'll never see any flowers growing outside again."

Mrs. Clay did not think the sick woman
would, and she was quite willing that her
little daughter should do as she pleased
with her daisies.

The box was carried carefully to Mrs.
Smith's the next morning, and it made such
a gleam of brightness in the dull room, and
gave the invalid so much pleasure, that
Sadie did not regret her self-denial.

But on the Thursday before the anniversary, when the little girl went to carry
Mrs. Smith some nice jelly that her mother
had made for her, she found the sick woman
asleep, while chubby Sam was industriously
picking the daisies to pieces, saying, " Pitty!
pitty!" every time he nipped off a blossom.
Sadie did not trust herself to speak; she put

18

down the jelly very quietly and ran home crying. Her mother comforted her as much as she could be comforted, and then she advised her to go and tell Mr. Mervale of her trouble.

"Well, little daughter," said the clergyman, kindly, when Sadie had finished her story, "your flowers have been just as acceptably offered to God as though they had helped to make our celebration beautiful."

The little girl looked surprised at this, but she soon came to understand what Mr. Mervale meant when he talked to her of honoring Christ our Lord through his sick and suffering servants. She went home happier than she had expected to feel and trying not to envy the pleasure and the triumph of her companions.

Very early that Sunday morning Sadie was up, and on going down stairs a scream from Bridget drew her to the front door.

"Did ye iver see the likes o' that?" said the Irish girl as she lifted from the porch a pot of callas—two beautiful blossoms and one creamy bud. "Shure, the Blissid Vargin herself sent 'em; she loves the lilies."

"No, Bridget, God has sent them," replied the little girl, reverently, as she carried her prize into the parlor.

The pot was placed just as it was among the other floral offerings, and, banked up with soft green moss from the woods, the lilies looked so beautiful that Sadie felt, while puzzling over the gift, no one need desire anything more appropriate.

Mr. Clay could probably have told how the lilies found their way to his front porch, but it was a long time before he had anything to say on the subject.

"How nice he was!" said Clara, rapturously. "And it's such a pretty story altogether! But what did make you think of a cherry-colored cat, Miss Harson?"

"I did not really think of it 'all out of my own head,'" was the smiling reply, "but a long time ago I heard of a man who pretended to exhibit a cherry-colored cat; and when people had paid their money to go in and see it, he showed them a common black cat and said that black was the color of some cherries."

"He was a wicked man, then," said Edith, who seemed to feel as much injured as though she herself had been imposed upon.

"He certainly was, dear," replied her governess, "and I have no doubt that he was punished for it; for the Bible tells us that 'the way of transgressors is hard.'— But of what is little Janey thinking so deeply?"

"Of all the beautiful things you told us," said the child, "and that Sadie offered her daisies to God when she gave 'em to the sick woman."

Miss Harson could see that the little girl was taking comfort over her own spoiled lily and trying to offer it in the same way.

CHAPTER XVIII.

CONVALESCENCE.

WHEN the beautiful spring weather came, at last—bright with flowers and birds and sunshine—the two little invalids were quite out of the hospital, declaring that they felt "as good as new" again. They were not quite so good as that, though, and little Edith needed a great deal of care for a long time afterward. But they were not ill any longer, and this was certainly great cause for rejoicing. It was pleasant, too, to think that while amusing themselves they had made a number of pretty little gifts for the sick children at the real hospital, and it was not easy to tell which had most pleasure in these gifts, the children who received them or the children who gave them.

"Kind friends seem to be constantly thinking of the sick little ones," said Miss

Harson, "and preparing beautiful surprises for them; and when we remember the loving words of our Saviour, 'Inasmuch as ye have done it unto the least of one of these, ye have done it unto me,' they should make us feel what a privilege it is to work for his poor and suffering children."

"And wasn't it nice, Miss Harson," said Clara, "to see how surprised Janey was at her scrapbook that she had made herself, and the picture, too—which she always loved so much—that you gave her?"

That bright, happy little face, so full of intense surprise as its owner gathered up her treasures, could not easily be forgotten, and never in her short life had Janey felt so rich. It was so kind, she thought, of the dear young lady to give her that beautiful picture of "The Good Shepherd," to hang up in the little room at home for her very own; and, as to the scrapbook, how could she ever have supposed that she was the little girl for whom she was making it? It was just too lovely! Janey almost felt as if she were dreaming, except that the things

were there to show that it was all real, and
people never get the things they want in
dreams; so the little girl went home on
that Saturday afternoon with more thanks
in her heart than she had been able
to express with her lips, and with the
precious gifts held as tightly as though
she had expected them to be snatched
away from her.

"Being sick has left some pleasant
marks, I think," said Miss Harson, "although all signs of measles have long ago
disappeared. And thinking of others is always the best way to get rid of complaining thoughts. I wonder if my little girls do
not agree with me?"

"Yes, dear, dear Miss Harson," was the
earnest reply from both of the children as
Edith nestled closer; while Clara lovingly
twined her arms around her governess as
she added,

"It has been so pleasant to work for the
hospital, and to teach Janey, that we almost
forgot we were sick."

"There ought to be three Misses Harson," said Malcolm, from the doorway,

"for no one leaves *me* even a little piece of this one to get hold of."

The young lady laughingly stretched out her hand to him, and, bowing low over it in knightly style as he kissed it, Malcolm continued quite soberly :

"I came to ask a favor which Clara and Edith are both too bashful to speak of; they said they never would have thought of doing such a thing. Will you not please tell us a story ?"

The little sisters laughed merrily at the idea of their being bashful on this point, and their governess replied that, knowing what insatiable children she had to deal with, she scarcely dared ever to be without a story of some kind.

"But what shall it be, Malcolm ?" she continued. "Shall it be of some one who started out with grand resolutions to do everything that was lofty and good, but failed because he trusted in his own strength? or shall I tell of some humble and timid soul that gained the victory through faith ?"

There had seemed to fall a thoughtful

silence on the little flock in that Saturday
twilight, and the young governess, who so
dearly loved them all, had sometimes feared
that of the bright, generous-hearted boy beside her it might be written, " Unstable as
water, thou shalt not excel."

" Tell us of the last one," said Malcolm,
hastily, with a half-conscious color on his
face. Sometimes he almost saw one of
the little foxes that spoiled his grapes.

"And it's going to be all your own story,
isn't it, Miss Harson?" asked Edith.

" Yes, dear, all my own story; and perhaps you will think it too serious, but I want
you to like it. The name of my story is

"CLEAN AND WHITE.

" ' Now the other foot, darling ; mamma's
baby must be all clean and white for Sunday, you know.'

" ' Mamma's baby' was a mischievous-
looking little sprite with great blue eyes
and rings of golden hair, and, wriggling
her little pin-cushion of a foot so that
mamma had some trouble to get it into
the basin, she laughed and crowed in great

glee at the disturbance she was making. She was nearly two years old, and mamma would have said that she was 'just the cunningest baby that ever lived.'

" 'All white and clean,' continued the cheerful voice, 'to greet the day on which our Lord rose from the dead, with all the gloom of the grave past and gone. Oh, Baby, it is easy enough to make the body clean and white, but would that you could keep your little white soul as it is now!'

" ' Will you not tell me what that means?' said a voice that seemed to come out of the shadows.

" The twilight was fast deepening, but, busy with her baby, Mrs. Ford had not noticed that it was lamplighting-time. The words startled her, and she could just distinguish the grocer's boy with a basket on his arm. She had seen him before, and knew that he was small of his age and not over-strong; but his days were filled with work, for all that, and on this Saturday afternoon he had been hurrying back and forth until his legs fairly ached.

" Tom liked to go to Mrs. Ford's; she

always had a pleasant smile for him, and sometimes a cake or a Sunday-school paper. It looked like home there, too, though it was only a small wooden house—one of the plainest in town; and Mrs. Ford lived there alone with little Alice and did her own work, besides a great deal of fine sewing for the grand ladies of the place. Her husband had been a sailor, and about a year before this the sad news had come that his ship was lost with all on board.

"'What it means?' repeated the kindly little woman when Baby Alice had been safely stowed in her night-dress. 'Why, it means that beautiful day of the week that 'we call Sunday. Do you not go to Sunday-school, Tom?'

"'Yes'm,' was the reply; 'I goes to the mission school, but they doesn't tell us nothin' pretty like that there.'

"'But do they not tell you,' asked Mrs. Ford, 'about Jesus our Saviour, and how he came to live upon earth nearly nineteen hundred years ago, and how wicked men crucified him? But he died willingly that we might be saved, and on the third

day after he rose from the grave, and is
alive for evermore; and that is why we
keep Sunday with everything clean and
white. And we must not be afraid to die,
because Jesus has said that we shall rise
again as he did, and live with him in
heaven; and when God takes away those
whom we love, we must remember that
he is keeping them safe for us until we
can go to them.'

"Tom saw the tears in the soft eyes at
these last words, and that Mrs. Ford
glanced quickly over at little Alice, whom
she had placed in her crib, and who was
already asleep; but the boy thought more
of not being afraid of death—that vague
terror to him—than of parting with those
he loved, for he had none to lose, poor
fellow! and could not even remember his
father and his mother.

"'How would you like to spend the day
with me to-morrow, Tom?' asked Mrs.
Ford, after a few moments' thought. 'I
will get everything ready in the morning,
before I go to church, and leave you in
charge of Baby; then we will have a nice

little dinner, and in the afternoon I will take you and Alice to the Sunday-school, where the children have their anniversary to-day. You shall take tea with me, too, and then I will tell you more about Sunday. Shall you like it?'

"It sounded delightful to the lonely boy, whose Sundays were not very cheerful, and Baby Alice was such a dear little thing that he did not at all mind taking care of her.

"But how, wondered Tom, as he went to his comfortless bed in the grocer's attic, could he be 'all white and clean for Sunday'? He had not much that was white, and he was not at all sure about being clean; but he scrubbed himself with soap and water and laid out the best of his scant wardrobe to put on in the morning. How strange it seemed, though, that it should be raining on Sunday, when Mrs. Ford had said that it was always so bright! It was a light rain, to be sure, and made the grass look green, but Tom thought that it should not have rained at all.

"'Sunday does not depend for its brightness on the skies, Tom,' said Mrs. Ford;

'it is Sunday just the same even when it rains, and we must learn to forget about the weather.'

"The morning passed pleasantly, and Alice cried only once. This was when Tom took away from her a pretty shining pin, that she had contrived to get hold of with a great deal of trouble, just as she was putting it into her mouth to see if it tasted as good as it looked; but her young nurse soon quieted her with some pictures.

"It did not seem so very long before Mrs. Ford returned from church, and her face had a wonderful light in it as she told Tom of the beautiful service and how holy and clean all Christians should strive to be, within as well as without. 'Holy and clean'! There it was again! And the boy felt almost discouraged at the strange whiteness that seemed to linger about this first day of the week.

"The little table was daintily spread, with a vase of flowers in the centre. Snowdrops and violets, Mrs. Ford called them, but Tom only knew that the purple ones gave out a delicious fragrance and the white ones looked like 'holy and · clean.' The boy had never sat down to just such a dinner, and that little frame house was a sort of paradise to him.

"The anniversary in the afternoon was a fresh source of wonder, and Tom scarcely breathed, for fear of losing something that was said or done. Alice behaved beautifully, and the little party had a very happy time. Afterward came Mrs. Ford's promised talk, and Tom began to see what the 'white and clean' meant. The day was one to be remembered, and the boy went back to his attic with a lightened heart.

"On the next Lord's day Tom was lying in one of the little white beds of a hospital. No one seemed to know just how it happened, but in the grocer's cellar a heavy cask had rolled over on the boy's thigh and crushed it badly. The whole limb had to be amputated, and Tom grew weaker every day, until the doctors said that he could not live much longer.

"When the boy first came out of the long sleep into which he had been put with chloroform, and found himself in a clean white bed and in fresh, snowy clothes, he murmured dreamily, "White and clean! White and clean!'

"Mrs. Ford was sitting beside the cot, and she cried as she remembered how eager Tom had been, a week ago, to know the meaning of the Sunday whiteness; but he whispered smilingly,

"'I'm going to *Him*—him that you told me about—and he has promised to make me white and clean all over.'

"It was Tom's last Sunday on earth."

The children were quite still when Miss Harson had finished the story, and Clara and Edith were crying softly. Even Malcolm's voice was quite husky when he tried to speak, and their governess said gently,

"We will all strive to be clean and white within, that when the great Lord's day comes we may be fit to 'see the King in his beauty.'"

THE END.

www.ingramcontent.com/pod-product-compliance
Lightning Source LLC
Chambersburg PA
CBHW020854020726
47497CB00005B/1395